KNIGHTMARE'S GAME

Knightmare's Game

DAKOTA FRANDSEN

Copyright © 2025 by Dakota Frandsen and Bald and Bonkers Network LLC.
All rights reserved.

The Paranormal Raider Force, *Knightmares Among Worlds, The Ones Who Walk All Worlds: A Giant's Curse, The Ones Who Walk All Worlds*, and related products and services are copyrighted under the sole ownership of Dakota Frandsen.

The stories presented in *Knightmares Among Worlds*, including *Knightmare's Game* and *The Ones Who Walk All Worlds*, are works of fiction. Names, characters, places, events, and incidents are the product of the author's imagination or are used fictitiously. Any resemblance to actual persons, living or dead, business establishments, events, or locales is entirely coincidental.

While the events in this book and others in the series are loosely inspired by true stories, they are not intended to threaten, attack, harass, or negatively affect any individual or group. The author and publisher do not endorse any actions, beliefs, or views presented in the stories, as they are purely fictional and created for entertainment purposes. Any similarities to real-life situations are unintended and should not be construed as factual.
No part of this publication may be reproduced or transmitted in any form or by any means, electronic or mechanical, including photocopying, recording, or any information storage and retrieval system, without the prior written permission of the author and publisher.

First Printing, 2025

Contents

1	City of Angels?	1
2	Review of Eden's Shadow	11
3	Drip. Drip.	15
4	Drug Lords Going Missing	33
5	News Article on Suspicious Disappearances	39
6	What I Am...	43
7	Sky Light	55
8	The Beginning	69
9	A Stage for Aspiring Stars	73
10	Dream a Dream in Trees	77
11	Scarlett's Nightmare	81
12	The Dragon of Los Angeles	85
13	Alternate Realities	91
14	StarCulling	95
15	Truth and Reconciliation	117

Chapter 1

City of Angels?

It is just after dark in a Los Angeles diner, as the staff enjoyed a slow shift. Customers who visit Carrie's enjoy a traditional 50s atmosphere and award-winning food.

On an average day, the average patron will be greeted by teenage lovers, average business men, and occasional surprises from actors starting out and ones practically everyone can recognize. Every now and then, a representative of nearby music labels will attend weekly karaoke nights, hoping to find the next hopeful musician to seduce their ears.

Between the months of January and April, 1 the infamous pilot season, the diner is usually filled with prideful hopefuls in town looking for their chance to make it into the next big sitcom or be the next A-Lister so they can rub their winnings in the noses of all who doubted them. Perhaps that is a poor choice of phrasing.

However, this was still LA. A city of dreams in which anyone willing to put in exemplary work and find themselves on the generous end of Lady Luck can become something almost unrecognizable. As such, with any large grouping of sentient beings, less-than-desirable traits always find a way to come to the surface and permanently scar unfortunate onlookers. Perhaps that was why everyone grew tense when a rather large man in a black wool trenchcoat, red button-up shirt, dark jeans, and black steel-toed boots entered the diner for the fifth time this week.

It was hard not to imagine why the unsuspecting spectators would feel a bit intimidated as the man's frame seemed to fill the entire edge of the door. The top of which seemed close to scalping him was it not for his occasional habit of slouching. It was also probably a good thing the man had a cleanly shaven-head. The metal frame had a tendency to catch loose hairs in its static pull or within the tiny chips in the structure that reflected its age. Aside from his choice of clothing and Viking-like figure, there was not much to give anyone the impression the man was dangerous. Unless you were witness for maybe a couple of occasions where local gangsters harassing the waitresses suddenly acted more respectfully at the sound of the man clearing his throat.

KNIGHTMARE'S GAME ~ 3

A waitress emerged from the back of the diner. She pulls out a small notepad from one of the pockets in her apron as she follows the man. He is glimpsing through a folded-up newspaper he fetched from a stand next to the entrance. He walks over to a booth in the back of the diner. A common tactic to give him a private view of the place with minimal risk of an attack from behind. He moves his free hand below the gap of his jacket and brushes it upwards as he takes his seat.

"Can I get you anything, big guy?" she asked.

"How about that chicken BLT on white, some tots, and a coke?" the man suggested as he glanced at her nametag, "Thank you kindly, Ms. Scarlett."

"You know, you keep coming here and know my name, but yet I don't know yours?" Scarlett perked.

"David," the man smirked.

"Tell me then, you keep coming cause you want to get my number, or you looking for somebody?"

David glanced towards a clock just above the kitchen counter as one of the other servers reached for an elderly man's order of fresh apple pie and strawberry smoothie. His focus on the hands of the clock seemed to make it strain, inching closer, as David knew something was about to happen. The part that worried him most? The innocent lives that might get caught in the crossfire of a local gangbanger, compromised by the use of illegal narcotics, burst through the door with an H & K MP5K automatic pistol.

He fired a series of shots straight into the clock's face. The diner patrons all scatter and duck to avoid being struck by stray gun fire, all except David and Scarlett. Upon realizing the man's true intentions that burst into the diner, David burst from his seat, nearly breaking the table from the screws which held it to the tile floor. David quickly grabbed Scarlett and forced her underneath him as they fell into the booth. It was the only way to ensure she would be sheltered by his large frame. Scarlett's body tried to shake from the sudden shock of being in the middle of a shooting. However, she found herself hardly able to move under David's weight.

"Stay down until I get him out of the building," David muttered.

Scarlett would've found relief from the added pressures of a large man removing himself from on top of her. However, the shock of the incident still riddled her heart at dangerous rates. She watched, slowly feeling her mind regress to the state of a young girl. As she saw the kind stranger she happened to meet at work one time, grasp the backs of the closest stool near the counter and strike the assailant across the chest. The blow sent the attacker flying towards the metal door of the diner, nearly blasting it off its hinges. More deafening shots were fired as the trauma, and likely rib-shattering 6 smack forced the muscles in the attacker's arms and hands to seize. The injury rippled through the man's upper body, causing him to yank the trigger and fire more rounds into the ceiling. Scarlett watched in amazement that paralleled her fear. It was almost like she was witnessing a real-life superhero.

The diner's patrons gathered towards the front windows, hoping to catch a glimpse of the show. And what a show it was! David towered over the purple-haired, five-foot nine, one-hundred-sixty-pound attacker. He was not afraid to utilize the difference in size as he continued his brutal assault. It was hard for anyone to hear the conversation from inside the diner, except for one sentence David roared with inhuman rage.

"Where is Knightmare?!"

The attacker was hard to understand in his cries, but all who spectated knew without a doubt that an answer was not provided as the attacker screamed, "Go fuck yourself!"

Onlookers passing on the street realized what was unfolding. They began to take in the spectacle themselves, some taking out their phones to record all that was happening. One woman cried for someone to call the police, only to realize by the sounds of quickly approaching sirens that someone or something already did. Feeling as if he was being backed into a corner, David knew he would have to reveal a few other tricks he had up his sleeve. He closed his eyes, took a deep breath, and grabbed the attacker by the throat. David's nails dug into the man's flesh, drawing even more blood not shed from the earlier assaults.

As for the attacker's gun? It was rendered useless as the entire magazine was spent inside the diner, a move David had planned. The wind surrounding them emerged from nowhere and grew stronger. The sudden storm seemed in synch with the sudden distortions in the air that originated from David, like a mirage causing a desert highway to appear to flow like waves in the ocean.

"WHERE IS KNIGHTMARE?!" David roared louder.

"I don't know," pleaded the man as puddles of urine formed down his pants.

David, growing tired of the man's alleged ignorance, lifts him to eye level and tightens his grip. The automatic pistol falls from the man's grip and onto the asphalt by David's size 18 feet as David leans near the man's ear and whispers something. The distortion around him seemed to become more in tense. The wind blew stronger, police drew closer, and nearly all the spectators scram bled in fear. Some even felt afraid for the man, as clearly the danger was no match for the supernatural horror he was pissing off. Evidently, this was the case as the anger of the superhuman giant began to manifest as a consuming flame that started to burn the would-be robber from head to toe. The screams and pork-like smell of burning human flesh broke Scarlett free from her trance, and for reasons unknown to her, she ran outside, hoping to get David's attention.

"STOP IT!" Scarlett's scream echoed as tears began to pour from her eyes.

David's focus shifts to wards her, not realizing that he has gone into a state of utter focus, causing only a fraction of his abilities to emerge. Sudden guilt for causing Scarlett begins to fill his heart, and a blinding white light appears, dumbfounding all who witness it. Even the police became paralyzed by the light's magnificence as they emerged from their patrol cars. Minutes, which felt like hours, passed be fore the light suddenly disappeared. Those entirely blinded by it found all that remained was the would-be robber resting on his knees with his hands up in the air.

As tears rolled down the man's face, all witnesses to the violence became amazed when they realized the man's fresh wounds were completely healed. His physical condition was exactly as it was when he entered the diner. As for his weapon, the police quickly found that the parts necessary for the gun to fire were melted. As for Scarlett, she knew in her heart what she had seen but was too afraid to admit it. The police began to process the scene as another waitress ran outside.

"Scarlett, babe, are you alright?" she yelled, running to comfort her coworker.

"I don't know, Georgia," Scarlett choked, "What the hell just happened?"

While Scarlett was a beautiful 26-year old blonde Hollywood hopeful from Boise, Idaho. Georgia was a 54-year-old Los Angeles native. The pair was almost like a mother and daughter, a relationship that honestly caught them both by surprise. Georgia was an actress until one fateful night, she lost her husband and her then 8-year-old son in a car accident. The other driver in that accident was heavily intoxicated, ejected from the vehicle, and died on the scene. Georgia was the only survivor, forever marked with crippling memories of her family and sporadic seizures from the neurological damage she treated with prescription CBD oil.

The diner was a saving grace for her, a simple job that allowed her to have some money coming in on top of her disability. It also provided a reason to leave the house. When Scarlett came to town and got a job at the diner, Georgia perhaps saw a bit of herself in the young hopeful, which led to her offering up her late son's old room. Georgia was even kind enough to offer advice and aid to Scarlett whenever auditions came around.

At first, such a bond seemed strange to some until they learned that her son, Wyatt, would've been the same age as Scarlett. Georgia even joked that she could see Scarlett and Wyatt being a cute couple. Finding such a connection seemed hard to do in such a chaotic world. Little did they know that tie would be the one thing to help them cope with what was to come.

"I think," Georgia pondered, "I think that was the 'Dragon' guy from the news."

"What?" Scarlett shook her head, "What 'Dragon guy' are you talking about?"

Realizing that the young girl she considered a daughter was still in shock, Georgia wrapped her arm around Scarlett's shoulder. Then starts to lead her back inside the diner to wait for the police to question them. It was an overwhelming night for them all. A night that would've been even more frightening had they looked towards the sky to see a tall black and red figure watching them from the top of a nearby building. To her surprise, it was David.

Perhaps it was best that Scarlett and Georgia only realized much more was about to unfold when they discovered a business card and a note on the table David sat at. Still trying to process all they had just witnessed, they could only look once the first two words of the note were readable from a distance.

"I'm sorry."

The rest was a phone number, presumably to reach David when the dust had settled. Scarlett's mind became fixated on this night, and who could blame her. Who was this man? What did she just witness? These questions and more filed her mind as her, Georgia, and other diner patrons responded to the police's questioning. As much as she felt it was probably for the best to do so, Scarlett felt an unnatural compulsion to hide the business card from David away.

So much for the City of Angels...

Chapter 2

Review of Eden's Shadow

Review of "Kivuli cha Edeni" (Eden's Shadow) - A Multifaceted Gem in Los Angeles

Tucked away in a vibrant corner of Los Angeles, *Kivuli cha Edeni* (Eden's Shadow) stands out as more than just another nightclub—it's a grand entertainment complex that caters to nearly every conceivable need for its patrons. From those seeking a lively nightlife experience to families looking for a full day of fun, Eden's Shadow is a multi-faceted oasis that promises an unparalleled level of safety, luxury, and entertainment.

Ambiance & Atmosphere: The moment you step inside, it's clear that *Eden's Shadow* is designed for both relaxation and excitement. The bustling nightclub vibe is contained within walls that are anything but ordinary. The sound of the bass is powerful but not overwhelming, with music curated to set the mood without drowning out conversation. For those who prefer a quieter escape, the sound transitions smoothly into the high-end casino area where the clink of chips replaces the thumping bass.

Dining Experience: The five-star restaurant housed within *Kivuli cha Edeni* is undoubtedly one of its crown jewels. The menu, while exclusive, features innovative culinary creations from world-class chefs, providing a dining experience that is both decadent and diverse. However, be warned—reservations are notoriously difficult to get, which speaks volumes about the establishment's commitment to quality. Whether you're a foodie or just seeking a refined dining experience after a night of fun, this restaurant delivers.

Entertainment: Eden's Shadow knows that variety is key when it comes to keeping guests entertained. The theater stage plays host to top-tier performances, featuring Broadway-style productions and performances by well-known artists, all guaranteed to leave you awestruck. On the other side, amateur nights add a refreshing, local flavor to the venue, giving rising stars an opportunity to shine in front of a diverse audience. There's always something happening at Eden's, whether it's a high-profile concert or a surprise performance by a hidden gem.

Family-Friendly Features: One of the most intriguing aspects of *Kivuli cha Edeni* is its ability to balance the nightlife with family-friendly amenities. The adjacent hotel, spa, and pool area provide a luxurious escape for guests looking to unwind after a long day of festivities. Families will appreciate the arcade and the convenience of a hotel stay just steps away from the action. The environment is welcoming, and the fact that the venue actively caters to families while maintaining its allure for adults is a rare feat.

Safety & Security: While *Eden's Shadow* is packed with an electrifying atmosphere, it does not shy away from prioritizing the safety and comfort of its patrons. The management's commitment to providing a secure and welcoming space is evident in every detail. Bartenders are trained to spot potential issues, and their coordinated efforts with private security ensure that patrons can enjoy their time without fear. The presence of nursing staff for any medical emergencies further speaks to their attention to detail.

For law enforcement, *Eden's Shadow* extends special privileges, which enhances the already strong communication and cooperation between staff and public safety teams. This unique approach has been praised as an important step toward keeping the establishment a safe and enjoyable place for all.

The Owner's Vision: Owner Surtar Olsen is the mastermind behind this complex, and it's clear he has poured his heart and soul into making this place as inclusive and entertaining as possible. His dedication to providing a thrilling yet safe experience for all guests is visible at every corner of the establishment. Olsen's commitment to excellence shines through, and it's no surprise that patrons continue to return to Eden's Shadow for the ultimate experience in Los Angeles.

Conclusion: *Kivuli cha Edeni* (Eden's Shadow) is a spectacular and rare gem in Los Angeles' entertainment landscape. Offering a comprehensive experience that ranges from gourmet dining and live performances to family-friendly activities, this establishment stands apart as one of the most diverse and unique destinations in the city. With its emphasis on safety, luxury, and inclusion, Eden's Shadow manages to bring a wide array of experiences under one roof, making it a must-visit for both locals and tourists alike. If you're in the mood for a night out or looking for a getaway that has it all, Eden's Shadow is truly a place where you can lose yourself—and maybe find a little peace in the process.

Chapter 3

Drip. Drip.

Drip. Drip.

A young woman stands above a bath room sink, applying various bits of darkened or blackened makeup to contrast her unnaturally pale skin but match her charcoal hair. Her outfit donned a heavy metal band t-shirt with fonts illegible to anyone who wasn't a fan, black jeans that accented her natural curves with unnatural discomfort, and rainbow-highlighted sneakers. While usually the type to sit at home to watch some film on her computer or catch up on her schoolwork, she was somehow convinced to join her roommates for a night out after a rather embarrassing breakup from not one but two of her boyfriends. She was caught cheating, and the former men of her life ended up discovering each other after her grandmother revealed the truth.

"Come on, Jacquie!" one roommate shouted, "the guys are almost here!"

"Just a sec, Steph!" Jacquelin huffed.

As I said, she was the type who preferred to stay in the safety of whatever place she called home. Today, it was a five-bedroom house she rented a room from with four other young ladies.

Drip. Drip.

It wasn't the best-looking place. All the ladies in the house were beautiful twenty somethings who came to Los Angeles to pursue their careers.

Stephanie and Jacquelin happened to meet one day while registering for cosmetology school with hopes of be coming special effects artists. Stephanie, a bubbly and colorful young redhead, seemed the polar opposite of Jacquelin. As the saying goes, opposites attract. The two became quite close as they were often paired for massive assignments, total bodily overhauls notorious for requiring actors to stay completely still for hours on end. Their friendship blossomed further with the search for a place to stay.

Their most inner circle grew to a sisterhood of six upon dis covering the house they presently reside. Needing occasional maintenance, such as repairing a leaky bathroom faucet, it was the best they could afford. With a huff, Jacquie finally emerged from the restroom to be greeted by her eager "Girl Tribe," seconds away from leaving without her.

It was a welcoming gesture, especially as the thoughts were first conceived when the girls first met Abigail when her parents were thrown out. It was a tradition born from Stephanie's vibrant mind that any time someone in the house had their heart broken, a night out was to be spent! A judgmental pair, Abigail's parents, were, with mindsets akin to the days of old, couldn't adjust to the idea that their son wished to be their daughter.

It's not as if one would notice that there was once a time Abigail went by Alfred. A tall brunette figure disguised by an androgynous appearance was always outgoing and skilled in the arts. Her parents brushed off the flamboyant mannerisms as simple play time, even finding themselves chuckling at the variety of seemingly joyous outbursts. It was such warmness that Abigail eventually found a somewhat misguided strength to confess her true self. It is a situation that still haunted Abigail late at night. As time passed, she would find solace in her best friend turned romantic partner, Grace. Since they were children, Grace and Abigail had known each other, often mistaken as siblings because of their bond and similar appearance. Grace knew in her heart that Abigail was a bit different but accepted her nonetheless. That care and romantic affection saved Abigail's life during a suicide attempt long before they moved into the house.

The remaining two ladies were Mandy and Claire, foster sisters who pledged to always be in each other's lives as they were tossed out into the world by the system when they turned of age. Mandy was much like Jacquie in style and mannerisms, sticking towards either dark shades or bright rainbows that reflected the mood of their morning minds. Claire, on the outside, was practically the embodiment of the stereotypical blonde Barbie that all seemed to drool over. While genetics may have blessed her with such fine physical qualities, her MENSA-qualifying intellect forged her promising path to technical empires in Silicon Valley.

While all had their own reigns to grasp and paths to take, none of that mattered tonight. The night was simply sisters on the run from stress, ready to scream everything out, forget the world, and simply live.

Drip. Drip.

Outside, the girls could hear the horns of two topless BMWs wailing away as two eager young men hollered in unison. Even though the two gentlemen were respectful to the girls, enough for the ladies to call on them despite never actually dating, they were still men. Who could blame them for the excitement? After all, Jared and Jacob were attractive in their own right, and soon their nice cars would be packed full of gorgeous girls.

The ladies divided themselves between the cars, immediately letting themselves go in the moment as their arms flew to the air as the engines roared. Various pop songs accompanied their journey to one of the hot test nightclubs in Los Angeles. It seemed everyone even remotely interested in California nightlife would vacation just to see. Bright neon signs lit their path like gigantic fireflies in the night, guiding lost travelers to shelter until they came across the crystalline styles of "Kivuli cha Edeni," or Eden's Shadow.

If you weren't for mindless music and booze, the nightclub also housed a casino for betting men, a five-star restaurant with nearly impossible reservations, a theater stage with top-billed performances, and amateur nights for promising talents. For those too inebriated or tired to drive home, there was also a neighboring hotel, pool and spa, gym, and arcade for the little ones. The establishment prided itself on providing a safe and fun atmosphere for all.

No illegal substances were ever known to flow through its walls. Bartenders were trained to spot potential assaults with coded languages coordinated with private security to help get patrons safely home. There was even private nursing staff equipment with appropriate training to assist with any illness or injury on the premises. Most importantly, special entry and discounts were offered to members of law enforcement of any jurisdiction to sweeten the already open and cooperative communications in the event of unfortunate mishaps.

These and other staff perks, along with the openness and swiftness of response on behalf of the company, built a reputation for even the most paranoid and in danger of individuals to feel safe and at home. If home was the definition of a never-ending party to even the most "vanilla" of people, as the kids would say. The night progressed smoothly and with out fret for Stephanie, Jacquie, Mandy, Abigail, Grace, Claire, Jared, and Jacob.

Stephanie and Jacob occasionally drifted into their little world, teasing what the rest of the group already suspected was a blossoming love story. Abigail and Grace took the dance floor without a care for the fact neither possessed any coordination. Mandy and Jared opted to ease into the night's fun by trying their luck on slot machines. Claire and Jacquie relaxed in a private booth the group managed to secure for themselves using Stephanie's seemingly magical ability to persuade some bouncers to let them in.

"Don't you want to get out there a bit?" Claire shouted towards Jacquie, hoping to be heard over the music.

"What?" Jacquie screamed back.

"You should try to let off some steam. It's not healthy for you to bottle everything up!"

"Claire, I'm not ready."

"Jacquie, honey, it's their fault. Men can be assholes and sleep around, so why can't we?"

"You know it's my grandma who told them, right?"

"Bitch please, your grandma is just old! No one has just one fuck buddy anymore," she scoffed, "I bet she was a slut, too, when she was younger."

"CLAIRE!" Jacquie squealed in embarrassment, "No, just NO!"

Claire couldn't help but laugh. "Look, all I'm trying to say is that you need to move on with your life! Stop looking for every little excuse to sit on your fine ass and join the world! You will miss out if you continue to be a pathetic little bitch!" Claire preaches with her hands held in the air, "I know you hate when I talk like this, but you know I love you. But if you don't get up and embrace life, you might miss out on that big hunk that's been checking you out for the last five minutes!"

Jacquie became riddled with confusion. It wouldn't be the first time that Claire tried to rattle someone with her outspoken manner, but one thing she never seemed to lie about was when someone she found attractive was near. Jacquie took Claire's sudden jerks and spasms, adjusting her appearance as the definitive sign that someone was quickly on approach.

"Good evening, ladies," a husky voice muttered, "How is the evening treating you?"

Jacquie slowly looked up in the direction of Claire's astonishment. A tall man of a heavy build was resting a rather large hand on the back of the booth. Well dressed in a form-fitting, yet non-restricting, three-piece suit. The black tones and white button up shirt complimented the oak-scented cologne, appropriately groomed stubble, and freshly shaven head. The man didn't seem the type to be overly concerned about his looks. Still, he occasionally took time for personal grooming when the mood struck.

"Umm, we're doing okay," Claire nervously flirted, "I always get anxious seeing how many people come here."

"And this is a slow night," the man joked, "So if the large crowds make you nervous, what brings you two ladies in tonight?"

As the large man glances toward Jacquie with a playful smirk, Claire sighs.

"Girls' night, just to kill some stress," Jacquie answered.

"Oh, a girl's night! Wonderful, wonderful! So am I correct in assuming there are others here with you?" the man asked.

"Yeah, um, I was actually going to go find out where they went," Claire responded, "Can you hold our spot Jacq?"

Jacquie understandably tensed up as Claire got ready to leave their booth. Confused about what to do, the man stood back as Claire brushed against his body and noted a cheeky smirk plastered on her face.

"Some friend, eh?" the man remarked.

"She's ... well, I don't know what she is some days, to be honest," Jacquie sighed.

"Pardon my boldness in stating that she isn't quite a good friend," the man interjected.

"It's not like that. She just..."

"Puts on an act?"

"How did you know what I was going to say?"

"Again, pardon my boldness, but in running this place, you tend to run into all sorts of... interesting people," the man replied, "There's never a dull moment, but after a certain amount of time, one begins to notice patterns. People get predictable."

"So what, did you come over here to try hitting on me because you thought you 'noticed' something?" Jacquie quipped.

"Well, Miss Jacquie, as the owner and CEO of this fine establishment, I occasion ally walk amongst the people. Mingle a bit, catch a free show, that sort of thing. I did overhear you resisting the urge to smack Miss Claire."

Jacquie's face began to turn red at the man's remarks, slowly letting her guard down to want to comfortably continue the conversation. Upon realizing that Jacquie was too embarrassed to continue the discussion, the man quickly thought of an other quip hoping to sneak past an anxious woman's mental walls.

"Oh dear, clearly I was right," the man grinned, "Tell me, she suggested that you participate in a massive spank-bank orgy and film it?"

Jacquie lost control and became hysterical at the random joke. Her laughter echoed over the music, signaling to a leering Claire that her impromptu plot to land Jacquie another date was successful. The laughter even lured out the rest of her friends, curious to see the source of the commotion and sudden mood change. The man sat across from a suddenly cheery and extroverted Jacquie when all were gathered.

Not wanting to interrupt the two, the group took to the restaurant for a late dinner. Mandy took it upon herself to leave Jacquie a text message so they could all regroup and go home, but a sudden reply signaled they could all go home without her. Jacquie was going to be taken up to the owner's private penthouse, possibly for the night. None of them knew how the man could get Jacquie to let her guard down. The guys took it upon themselves to check into the owner to validate the claim and ensure their friend didn't fall for a false pickup line from an ambitious creep. When the employees they spoke to confirmed that the man was, in fact, the owner, Surtar Olsen (and despite his namesake being a fiery giant from Norse mythology, the man was quite kind), every one felt at ease and impressed. A combination that often lead to a "dream catch" in today's hookup culture.

On the way to the owner's private elevator, Jacquie's heart began to race as she noticed a lack of people. Yes, it was supposed to be the man's private penthouse, but the fact so many people came through the place as a whole made it seem like there wasn't some where that one could be alone.

"Hey, I know you said it was your penthouse, but how many people have access?" she pondered.

"That depends on the day, I suppose," he answered, "I do have my own office, which is what that light you see there is for..." As the two enter the elevator, Surtar points towards a faint light on the wall that is separated from the rest. "Basically, if I am available to chat in person, that light will shine green. Only management quarters have lights set up in the event they need my help with something, which is rare. They all have a phone number that bounces to the office and my cell when I am not in. Other than that, aside from a few emergency exits that might direct people through the penthouse if all other precautions fail, we shouldn't be bothered," Surtar added.

"Oh, okay," Jacq anxiously sighed, "Sorry, I'm just nervous."

"You're quite alright, dear. It's almost blindly obvious that your need to go out this evening was brought on by something rather upsetting," Surtar assured, "Bad breakup?"

"Yeah," Jacquie stressed, "And my family took his side."

"Ouch," Surtar cringed, "Well, how about this? I can whip us up a nice dinner, put something on the TV, and we can simply get to know one another better. Consider tonight simply a relaxing time with a new friend. If the night leads us to something more, so shall it be. Because quite frankly, if I may be honest, you are quite stunning."

Sudden blossoming blush on Jacquie's cheeks gave away her answer. It revealed the exit of at least most of her anxieties. The brief conversation and Surtar's charms were enough for Jacquie to be utterly oblivious to the enclosed space she was stuck in with some strange man. She knew it was prob ably not best to jump into a new relationship so quickly. Still, something about Surtar was just so enticing. Something exciting and mysterious about him made her throw out all logic and reason.

As the elevator doors opened, she was surprised by the view of a long hallway. A green light near one of the doors was enough evidence to reveal where Surtar's office sat. Much to her surprise, she couldn't hear the commotion from the nightclub below them. In fact, all she could hear were the hypnotic vibrations of an air pump underwater. Through the open window of the office, Jacquie could see colorful arrangements of various aquatic flora and fauna in a large fish tank.

Drip. Drip.

Surtar guided Jacquie towards another door at the hall's end, secured with a number pad and thumb scanner. Upon a successful entry of credentials, the door opened to a luxurious suite Jacquie had thought she'd only ever see in television shows. The living room was illuminated by a large television with the latest gaming consoles, security systems, and high-end satellite TV receivers. The structural designs were reminiscent of ancient civilizations, but Jacquie didn't know which one.

A kitchen area where Surtar began preparing the night's meal nearly glistened as if every appliance and crevice was brand new. Counters were arranged in a large U-shape to isolate the kitchen from the rest of the penthouse. Shelves of high-end alcohol were not far from the kitchen, with liquids still remaining, suggesting which were Surtar's favorites. Jacquie tried not to judge if someone was a drinker. Still, her previous experience with abusive partners made her a bit cautious.

"Oh, miss Jacquie, before I forget, do you have any food allergies I should know? Just to avoid any unnecessary hospital visits?" Surtar shouted.

"Just, uh, pineapples and strawberries," Jacquie told him. "I see. Good to know fruit kinks are off the table."

Jacquie's eyes widened, "WHAT?!"

"Just a joke! Promise! Feel free to turn on anything you like; make yourself comfortable!" Surtar replied, "Plenty to do up here! Hell, if you'd like, the jacuzzi is open. I keep a stash of bathing suits from the gift shop in the restroom that you are more than welcome to take home if you'd like. If none fit, I can get one that does!"

"Pushing your luck, aren't we?"

"Perhaps, but I wouldn't be here without taking a risk or two in life," Surtar grinned briefly before preparing the night's meal, "It should take about 45 minutes before dinner is ready."

As the night progressed, Jacquie became quite comfortable in the presence of a potential new lover. After all, the man was handsome, caring, ambitious, quite successful, and seemingly more considerate than most guys she knew. The smells of lemon, chicken, and a variety of spices that flew through the air from the kitchen made it a safe bet to assume he was quite the cook as well. As soon as the lemon chicken graced her tongue, the taste was almost as intoxicating as the white wine paired with it.

Being a twenty-something in California made it hard for her to have a quality meal that wasn't prepped and frozen beforehand, at least without exploiting herself to some nighttime hopeful gentlemen. With her guard down, masked by the delicious feast, all reason for her being suspicious was gone and made for what she considered one of the best nights of her life. Her comfort grew to the point she was open to ending this tale with a night of intense, passionate, and almost animalistic sex. And boy, with every twist and moan, every bit of saliva and spit, every thrust and squeeze, the pure ecstasy that filled Jacquie's body made her forget all her troubles. Each giggle and shout fueled her veins with body numbing tingles. Every shriek and scream of organismic release further satiated her hunger for sex.

Honestly, this was the most addictive and fulfilling sexual encounter she had known as hours passed by, with no recollection of the surrounding world, only the pulsating tastes of the most exciting man she had known. Towards the end of those hours, both Surtar and Jacquie fell asleep as Surtar's satin sheets barely covered their purely naked bodies.

By the middle of the night, just to run towards the little girls' room, Jacquie awoke, hardly able to walk. Her eyesight seemed to be having trouble adjusting to her surroundings, which wasn't something she was unfamiliar with, being that she was barely awake. Splashing water on her face helped her remember where she had spent the night. She subtly giggled as moments flashed before to remind her of the night's activities. She could hear Surtar talking in the other room as if he had received a rather serious phone call in the night.

'Probably just work related,' she thought as she splashed some more water on her face.

Surtar's voice seemed deeper than usual, probably just from him being half asleep still. Jacquie could hear him up and about, his voice creeping closer to the bathroom door. She stared, watching the bathroom door open, hopeful for a surprise continuation of her sex addiction's cravings. Her sight barely adjusted, her mind barely awake just in time for one final surprise. The surprise? Her face was bashed into the bathroom mirror by Surtar.

Jacquie fell to the floor, blood starting to frame her face a sit ran down her cheeks. Too stunned to move, shes oon realized what was about to happen. Surtar pulled the largest glass shard from the broken mirror and began to slice into whatever piece of Jacquie's flesh he could reach. Her arms, hands, legs, stomach, breasts, and back all took incredible amounts of pain. Jacquie would plead for her life, asking why Surtar would do such a thing, even bartering that she would not tell anyone what he did to her, all in a fruitless effort.

When Surtar stood tall and looked to wards the ceiling, Jacquie mustered what strength she could to try to run. Every part of her seemed cut, torn, and bruised, making every slight motion more excruciating than the first. Despite her condition, she was able to will herself forward. Salt from her tears burned the cuts to her now mangled face. If one unfortunate soul could see her, one that perhaps could've saved her, she was barely recognizable as the woman she was before. She had a fight left in her, and she was ready to do whatever it took to save her own life. But as the ferocious strength of a large, blood-lusting man's arms grabbed her, she knew it was too late.

She tried to thrash about, landing blows too weak to rattle her attacker. To Surtar, this entire event was hilarious. The pure adrenaline that flowed through his veins made the ecstasy he secretly slipped into Jacquie's food and drinks seem like nothing but a light buzz.

"You know," Surtar growled in Jacquie's ear, "The friends that left you here with me are about to die too. Just enough will be left for whatever excuses for a family you have so they can have their funerals for you all, but no one will ever know the truth about what happened to you. No one will know you were here. You will be nothing. Sure I may find some use for your bodies, but you will still be nothing. You are nothing!"

The words might've had a chance to torment Jacquie, but the feel of a man's teeth gripping her throat and silencing her scream was what it finally took for her mind to completely disassociate. Her shock saved the fear of rapid blood loss and the tear of flesh from her body as it was devoured by Surtar.

She could see everything happening to her, but no longer from the perspective of her own eyes. She could feel phantom sensations still, a sign that some part of her was still alive. Something she wished was not true as she watched Surtar put his right hand on the wound in her neck and thrust downward. Was she somehow able to become conscious again, the loud snap was all she needed to know that she would be permanently paralyzed.

"Oh my god, Jacquie!" screamed a familiar voice. Jacquie turned around to see that Stephanie, Claire, Mandy, Grace, Abigail, Jared, and Jacob were all in similar conditions as her. All were too dumbfounded to truly know what happened, only to be clued in by their sudden ability to move through the wall. Surtar stood from Jacquie's naked and mangled corpse, proud as ever of his accomplishment. He started to walk towards the kitchen and grabbed a towel to wipe the blood from his mouth, a meat cleaver, and a sharpened ice cream scoop before returning to the corpse.

"What the fuck are you doing, you sick son of a bitch?!" yelled Jacob.

Surtar squatted next to Jacquie's head, wiping the stray hair away from her face. He looks at the eight spirits in the room and smiles. "Recycling," he jokes.

Surtar used the sharpened scoop to remove Jacquie's eyes from her sockets. Then, he completely decapitated the corpse with one fell swoop of the meat cleaver. The eight spectral friends watched in horror, wanting to vomit with non-existent organs.

Drip. Drip.

The following morning the neighbors of the six ladies were awakened by the screams of police securing an unspeakable scene. A concerned elderly couple came over to check on the ladies after hearing some commotion overnight. Naturally, they had assumed that one of the ladies was upset over another breakup. What was discovered, though, gave the elderly couple a heart attack. What was later found by another concerned neighbor nearly did the same. What was located on the inside of the house were seven severed heads, all displayed with jaws open and eyes placed on what remained of their tongues. What was discovered on the wall behind the skulls even shook the veteran detectives and forensic crew on the scene. One of the detectives reached into the inner chest pocket of his jacket to pull out his smartphone, immediately dialing the one number belonging to who he needed most on this case.

"David, it's me. He's killed again."

Drip. Drip.

That sound seemed to echo through the house from the message left on the wall, in what all could only assume was fresh blood.

Drip. Drip. Come and Play.

Chapter 4

Drug Lords Going Missing

The Mysterious Disappearances and Deaths of Drug Lords: A Hidden Crime Wave?

A chilling pattern is emerging in the world of organized crime: several high-profile drug traffickers and cartel leaders from across North America have vanished without a trace or been found dead under eerie, ritualistic circumstances. These events have raised alarms in law enforcement and among criminal insiders, as what initially seemed like isolated incidents may point to something far darker—a covert group systematically infiltrating and eliminating drug trafficking rings.

The Disappearance of Crime Lords

In the past few months, multiple notorious figures within the drug trade have mysteriously disappeared, leaving their empires in disarray. The first disappearance occurred in late summer, when Javier "El Diablo" Cortés, a feared kingpin linked to the Sinaloa cartel, vanished from his heavily guarded compound in Mexico. Days later, his body was discovered in a remote desert location, dressed in ceremonial garb, with his hands bound and eyes wide open.

What appeared to be a simple cartel feud quickly spiraled into a pattern when two other major figures, Victor Reyes, a Colombian drug lord, and Elena "La Bruja" Delgado, a key player in the Mexican drug trade, also went missing. Both of their bodies were discovered in ritualistic poses, their bodies mutilated in a manner that bore striking similarities to ancient religious rites, with symbols carved into their flesh.

The Ritualistic Murders

At first, law enforcement officials suspected that rival cartels or gangs were behind the murders. However, as more bodies turned up under similar circumstances, a more sinister theory began to emerge: someone—or something—was targeting and eliminating major crime figures.

Authorities have noted that the killings share chilling similarities to ritualistic killings seen in cult activity. The victims' bodies have been found arranged in strange, almost symbolic formations, with particular emphasis on ancient spiritual symbols, animal sacrifices, and bizarre markings. These deaths, seemingly tied to a group with knowledge of occult practices, have left both law enforcement and criminal insiders scratching their heads.

In one case, the body of a prominent drug kingpin was discovered in a remote forest, surrounded by burning candles and strange artifacts. Local investigators have suggested that the murders may be part of an underground group, someone working from the shadows to take control of the drug trade using fear, ritual, and precision.

The Emergence of the Unknown Group

The most unsettling development is the emerging theory that these ritualistic killings are not the work of rival cartels, but of a highly organized and secretive group that is systematically taking over the drug trade from within. This organization, which remains a mystery to both law enforcement and the criminal world, appears to be using a combination of psychological warfare and occult symbolism to assert dominance.

"Every crime lord that has gone missing or turned up dead under these circumstances was deeply entrenched in the drug trade," said one anonymous source close to a cartel. "These aren't random acts of violence. This group knows exactly what they're doing, and they're taking control of a dangerous, lucrative industry from the inside out."

Some have speculated that this group could be a modern-day version of a secret society or cult, one with deep knowledge of the occult and ancient rituals. Their methods appear to be an attempt to intimidate and subjugate the existing criminal power structures by using ritual killings to send a clear message: their reign is over.

The Cartels Fight Back

In response to these mysterious disappearances, drug cartels and criminal syndicates have begun to work together to investigate the killings. While traditionally known for their brutal and lawless behavior, cartel leaders are now desperate to understand the threat posed by this unknown faction. There have been reports of cartel leaders seeking occult experts, mystics, and even former cult members to decipher the ritualistic symbols left behind at crime scenes.

Some within the criminal community believe that these murders are a form of power struggle—a quiet war being waged against the cartels by a new, unidentifiable force. As these killings continue, it is feared that more cartels will crumble under the pressure, with power shifting into the hands of this mysterious, possibly dangerous new entity.

Law Enforcement's Dilemma

Law enforcement is under increasing pressure to solve these cases, but the ritualistic nature of the killings makes it difficult to pinpoint a motive or identify the perpetrators. Traditional crime-solving techniques aren't equipped to handle cases involving the occult, and the cartel's secrecy and reluctance to cooperate with authorities have made the investigation all the more challenging.

"The group behind these killings is highly sophisticated, and their motives seem to go beyond money or power," said Detective Laura Collins, who is working on the case. "There's an element of fear and control, but we don't have enough information to say for sure who or what they are."

A Growing Conspiracy

The true scale of this emerging conspiracy remains unclear, but one thing is certain: the underworld is facing a threat it has never seen before. The deaths and disappearances of these drug lords suggest that this secretive group is not just targeting individuals—they are systematically dismantling the structure of global drug trafficking from within, using fear, occult rituals, and calculated violence as their weapons.

As the investigation unfolds, one question lingers: who are these mysterious figures, and what do they want with the criminal empires they are dismantling?

With each new disappearance and death, the dark underbelly of the drug trade grows more unstable, and a chilling new power begins to rise from the shadows.

Stay tuned for further updates as this terrifying mystery continues to unfold.

Chapter 5

News Article on Suspicious Disappearances

Mysterious Disappearances Linked to New Age and UFO Events Across North America

Authorities across the United States and Canada are investigating an alarming pattern of disappearances tied to individuals traveling to New Age and UFO-related events. Over the past year, dozens of cases have been reported, with victims vanishing en route to conventions, retreats, and gatherings exploring alternative spirituality and extraterrestrial phenomena.

A Growing Concern

Law enforcement agencies have confirmed at least 45 cases involving missing persons who were last seen traveling to events in states like Arizona, California, and Colorado, as well as Canadian provinces including

British Columbia and Ontario. Many of these events center on topics such as UFO sightings, alien abductions, meditation practices, and energy healing.

The disappearances have raised concerns among families, investigators, and the broader New Age and UFO communities. While no concrete link has been established between the cases, some experts suggest there may be an organized effort targeting attendees of these events.

Shared Patterns

Victims share commonalities that have intrigued investigators. Many were active in online forums or social media groups dedicated to New Age spirituality or UFO research. Several reportedly received invitations to exclusive "secret" gatherings or claimed they were on the verge of uncovering groundbreaking information about extraterrestrial contact.

Witness accounts suggest that many victims were last seen leaving rest stops, gas stations, or small-town diners, often in remote areas. In some cases, their vehicles have been recovered, abandoned with no sign of struggle or personal belongings missing.

Family Pleas and Theories

Family members of the missing are desperate for answers. "My sister was so excited about this retreat," said Monica Espinoza, whose sibling, Vanessa, disappeared on her way to Sedona, Arizona. "She believed she was going to connect with like-minded people and learn something extraordinary. Now, we have no idea where she is or if she's safe."

Speculation about the cause of these disappearances runs rampant. While some suspect criminal activity, including human trafficking or cult involvement, others within the UFO community believe the incidents could involve government interference or even extraterrestrial abductions.

Official Responses

Law enforcement officials caution against jumping to conclusions. "We are actively investigating these cases, but there's no definitive evidence connecting the disappearances or tying them to UFO or New Age events," said Detective Morgan LaSalle of the RCMP's Missing Persons Unit.

However, some organizers of New Age and UFO events are stepping up security measures in response to the growing concerns. "We want to ensure our attendees feel safe and supported," said Dana Grant, a spokesperson for the Galactic Convergence Conference. "These disappearances are troubling, and we're working with authorities to assist in any way possible."

Online Communities in Turmoil

The online communities devoted to New Age and UFO phenomena are abuzz with speculation, fear, and solidarity. Some users claim to have received strange messages or warnings, while others are organizing their own search efforts.

"Something is going on, and it's bigger than we realize," one user wrote in a popular UFO forum. "People don't just vanish like this without leaving any clues. Getting people to actually find them instead of just jumping on the bandwagon will be next to impossible though."

A Call for Vigilance

Authorities are urging individuals planning to attend such events to take precautions, including informing family or friends of their travel plans, avoiding secluded areas, and remaining vigilant of their surroundings.

As the mystery deepens, the families of the missing are left with more questions than answers. For now, the New Age and UFO communities continue to grapple with an unsettling possibility: that the search for truth might have led some to disappear into the unknown.

Chapter 6

What I Am...

All Hands One Love Church was a sort of "new age" approach to religion, with a mission in mind that many mocked openly. That mission? To unite all faiths, no matter how foreign or recognized, under one banner to spread simple care for each and every person.

The founder, Gregory Mills, believed that all peoples were lost in one way or another. He felt that all people were merely trying to find understanding in a chaotic world. To combat this, to attempt to unify all people, Mills took it upon himself to build a library of books with all manners of faith so one can freely explore the world at their own leisure. He could develop his dream much further than he had anticipated. Much to anyone's surprise, he was quick to gather a following.

There were regular sermons in which Mills took lessons from all the various texts and reimagined them in the modern tongue. One could argue this was the source of Mills' success as it allured hundreds, if not thousands, to his steps when rumors began to swirl of an alleged supernatural vigilante being a frequent visitor. Some who came to realize that David Dragan was indeed the driving force that frightened the Los Angeles criminal underground advised that not taking up some secret identity was probably not the wisest move. After all, innocent people were caught in the middle of his battles because some thug recognized him.

For David trying to hide who he really was seemed irrelevant due to his large stature. Those who did recognize him knew all too well the potential chaos he could unleash. They were either upon the receiving end of David's might or the endangered innocent David was trying to help. Gregory had an apartment just above the church, which allowed him to be close by for whoever was in need. Security cameras connected to a smart home device help monitor the premises with almost nonexistent blind spots. This would allow him to monitor everything from his mobile device and set up what times he would want alerts to be brought to his attention.

Usually, this was simply part of his nightly routine or when ever he would leave to take care of matters elsewhere. Volunteers would help operate the stations 24/7, as well as private night security hired by a generous member after some teens broke in one night looking for a quiet place for sex. No charges were ever filed, but the tense emotions of a place of worship 48 being vandalized had no other way of being subdued. On this particular morning, Gregory gathered a few materials to attend a PTSD support group he hosted in the church's basement. It was the best place he could offer for all who attended to reflect with minimum distractions and occasional food and beverage to comfort the willing hearts.

A notification on his phone sounded off, signaling that the motion sensors picked up activity in the basement. Aside from a couple windows a person of childlike proportions could squeeze through, the only ways into the basement were through the main stairwell and elevator. Gregory pulled out his phone and tapped on the notification to see what triggered the sensor. He quickly grabbed the bags full of drinks and snacks as he realized that a large figured man was materializing on camera through a distortion in the image. He started setting up chairs for the support group.

To Gregory, this was a sign that the most famous and potentially most dangerous member of his "congregation" was once again active in his crusades, and some thing almost went wrong. David's brooding manner supported this notion nearly every time. The giant of a man glanced towards the security camera and grinned, "You coming down any time soon?"

Gregory shook his head and hurried to wards the elevator, meeting David right as the elevator doors opened.

"David!" he screamed, "Stop doing that!"

"Greg, I thought you might need some help carrying everything," David smirked.

Greg, shaking his head with a broken breath, handed David a bag with fruits, veggies, and two cases of soda to carry down stairs. "And you wonder why people like you were hunted as witches," Greg joked.

"Safe to say there hasn't ever been some one quite like me," David fired back, "At least no one that's alive."

"Yeah, yeah," Greg replied as he pressed the button in the elevator, "So what do I owe the pleasure?"

"What? I can't come to church just be cause?"

Greg shot David a glare.

"Fair enough," David sighed, "I came close to losing control again and almost killed a girl."

"Oh..." Greg realized, "What happened with this one? I assume this has some thing to do with the diner in this morning's paper?"

David nodded.

"You're not a bad person, David. The things you can do are scary but special all the same. You haven't killed anyone. I know you've done your best to at least physically heal anyone you've hurt. I'm sure that while this girl is probably shaken, whatever you had to do was to protect her," Greg rambled with his almost scripted advice, "You're nothing like your father."

"I know. I just can't shake the feeling sometimes," David nearly whispered.

"Did your dad even have your powers?" Greg asked.

"Kinda," David answered, "These things are genetic. But I'm the first, for some reason, who became this strong."

"There's probably a reason for that," Greg smiled, "Now, who was the girl? Anybody in particular?"

"She was a waitress who happened to be working when the gunman came in."

"Blonde? Pretty?"

David glared at Greg, knowing what he was insinuating.

"Yes," David admitted, "It was a bit frightening how much she looked like..."

"You're fiancé..." David pauses and waits for the elevator doors to open before proceeding. The loss of Skylar, his fiancé, brought him to Los Angeles in the first place. Not to escape his heartbreak and begin anew but to kill the person responsible. If only he knew the truth.

"It shows growth that you could share this with me in private. But, maybe, you will be able to heal more if you spoke more openly about it," Greg added. David looked around the large under ground recreation room in the church's basement. At the time, not much was in place, leaving it to be not much more than a storage room. The space was outfitted with secret access points that Greg would use to help hide people looking to escape abusive situations.

David knew of the safe rooms and the lengths Greg went to keep them fully operational after he tracked down a young girl who ran from a sexually abusive father. It was a moment in which David saw, for the first time, a kindred spirit looking to help save the world in what ways he could. It was a moment David finally found a friend.

"Greg, you know I respect you as a friend and a brother. I know you're right," David sighed, "But I don't know if that is a risk I can take."

"What do you mean?" Greg pushed, "No one here is going to share what you tell them. You're the reason many of them come here in the first place!"

"I never did explain it to you, did I?"

"No, you haven't. I figured you were stalling."

"In a way, I was," David admitted.

Greg shook his head with excitement, expecting that he may finally be breaking through David's emotional walls. His eyes widened, revealing to David all he needed to know without resorting to his supernatural resources. David glanced towards a clock on the southern wall and noticed about a fifteen-minute window to reveal a secret.

"You know how I can read minds, right?" David asked.

"Is there anything you can't do?" Greg replied.

"Actually, I'm not a very strong swimmer," David joked, "But that's not the point."

"Yes, I've caught on. What about it?"

"You ever wonder how that works?"

"I just thought..." Greg paused, "Not really.

"Not many people do. It's not much different from watching or listening to the radio. Our minds can act like broadcasting stations, and the body's own heat can reflect what's being played like speakers on a radio," David explained, "It happens with every living creature. Planets, stars, they all do it too."

"So, you're saying that anyone can do the things you do?"

"In a way, yes. Humans are still very much like infants in their potential," David smirked, "But as most who work with kids can tell you, every now and then, one comes along that's a little too smart. Everyone has some theory for it, from autism to the soul being from another planet..."

Footsteps echoed with the jingles of bells strapped to the church's side entrance leading to the basement. Hesitation filled nearly every step, telling the men there was about to be a new member. David shut his eyes to help focus his attention on his "other" senses. Most assumed that David's abilities were "just there," never considering how they worked. The veil of confusion added to David's effectiveness when it mattered most. Most would find themselves confused to hear that his powers were just extensions of his person. David's powers alter the world's senses as one's world is shaped, observed, and cataloged by the many senses that form the human mind. Such an example awaited as the image of a large man suddenly vanished before yet another familiar face made a surprise appearance.

"H...hello?" a nervous woman rattled, "Am I early?"

"Just a little, miss," Greg sighed, "But that's quite alright."

Greg walked towards a young blonde woman who practically radiated anxiety to welcome her to the support group.

"Oh, sorry, I guess I was just nervous about coming. I, um..." the woman stuttered.

"By any chance, would you be Scarlett? Scarlett Argyris?" Greg asked.

Scarlett clutched her purse tight. Tiny jewels clatter against the metals of the purse, forcing David's heart to race as he stood in the shadows. The dust that gathered was irritating to most sinuses.

"Yes," Scarlett answered quickly, "Are you, Pastor Gregory?"

"Yes, dear. And, please, you can call me Greg."

"Can I ask you something then, Greg?" Scarlett muttered, "I read online that the vigilante that's been in the news can be found here. The Dragon... or something. Is it true?"

"Miss Argyris, I can tell you this," Greg smiled, "The people who call him that aren't the ones you may want to associate with."

Scarlett grew confused.

"David!" Greg shouted, "It's rude to spy."

As if he knew David would not disappear from the view of this woman, Greg's voice struck David's nerves. A man with powers beyond understanding was riddled with nerves about meeting a woman he had saved yet again. A woman whose visual image re minded him of a once peaceful time that met a gruesome end. David swallowed his pride, took a deep breath, and stepped into view.

"Hello, Ms.," David said quietly, "I'm surprised to hear that you've been looking for me."

If it were possible to quantify the impact of self-consciousness, David felt in that moment, some may find little surprise to see Scarlett's eyes would likely correlate in size. She was accustomed to those. But seeing the figment of the supposed dreams standing before her was all the evidence she needed. Perhaps part of her was convinced that night in the diner was merely a strange nightmare. That night was no dream, it did happen, and people came close to death right before her very eyes. The one thing to stop it all, the crushing weight that likely saved her life, was now standing just twelve feet before her.

David knew that look, thus prompting him to speak up. "Did I hurt you the other night?" he questioned her.

"Um, no, no, no! It's okay," Scarlett muttered, "Just some bruises from the booth, nothing serious."

David moved towards her in utter silence, barely the whisper of breath leaving his nose. His hand nearly cradles Scarlett's arm as David shuts his eyes. A warm, somewhat welcoming glow emanated from his hands and seemed to seep into Scarlett's skin. David's touch was one of comfort, perhaps even love, making it so

Scarlett instinctively knew she had nothing to fear. A tingle radiated through her nerves, and pressure from her bruises seemed to lift. As David re leased Scarlett's arm, she rolled her cotton sleeves to find her bruises were seemingly just erased.

"How did you..." Scarlett muttered.

"I stimulated your body's metabolic processes to speed up recovery," David whispered.

"Okay, seriously," Scarlett jumped, "What are you?"

Greg stood in awe as it seemed space it self bent between David and Scarlett. Flickers of golden light broke through the veil of air. As they dissipated, Scarlett's cheeks began to brighten.

"What I am..." David muttered, "I'm just a guy with a few tricks up his sleeves."

The flick of David's smile and careful wink penetrated the inner walls of Scarlett's paranoia. Gregory had seen David's charm soothe the traumatized and fearful before. It was a useful trick which helped the recovery of many. It was a war David fought against the criminal underground, and no war goes without innocent casualties. David served as a holy flame in seemingly eternal darkness for many.

However, a different sort of heat was sprouting at that moment; one David thought he had lost forever. Perhaps, even David started to feel a sense of hope he had long lost. Greg could almost hear the strain of muscle on David's face as a smile began to form, followed by the immediate collapse and growl brought by the frustration of a ringing cell phone.

David reached into his pocket, sighed, and answered without uttering a single word.

"David, it's me," a voice echoed through the phone, "He's killed again."

The fortress of David's soul rebuilt its walls, his skin began to glow, and the air around him again seemed to ripple.

"I'll be there soon," David growled as he hung up the phone.

Screams of anger and frustration reverberate from David's mind. Sensing the disturbance, Scarlett grew afraid of what could happen next. Her breaths grew rapid and rattled. Knowing that his power was frightening the woman he had just healed, David took a deep breath and looked her in the eyes.

"Listen," he whispered, "I know you have many questions. You have my word that I will answer as many as I can. But right now, I need to go. Something worse than what you saw at the diner has happened, and I need to go."

"Are you okay?" Scarlett questioned.

David tilted his head to hide the tears that started down his face. Before he could answer, he teleported from the room, leaving Scarlett frozen in shock. Greg rested his hands on her shoulders for comfort and guided her to a chair in the next room before taking a seat himself.

"What's going on?" Scarlett asked him.

"Sweetie," Greg sighed, "War."

Scarlett growing ever more confused, started to get up and walk out, too over whelmed with what she just saw to focus. Greg watched her stride, noticing she grew more hesitant with every step. She wanted to leave, but something compelled her to search for more answers. Greg cleared his throat to catch her attention as she started back up the stairs.

"If you leave," he shouted, "You'll only allow yourself to be hammered by even more questions than you already have."

Scarlett stopped. She knew Greg was right; she would only be more haunted by glimpses of what she had already seen. She needed to know. She needed to know the truth for reasons beyond even her understanding.

"It's okay, Mommy," a mysterious little girl cheered, "They will keep you safe."

Scarlett looked at the phantom girl, nodded, and walked back to the chairs where Greg sat.

"You didn't tell me you had a daughter," Greg mentioned.

"It's... uh, long story."

Chapter 7

Sky Light

February 2015.

Long before the City of Angels became the battleground for modern superheroes, David was a young man from a small town in Idaho. A young man with abilities that frightened most, but a young man still. He was born here, molded here, awakened here. David's family was strongly affiliated with several emergency service agencies across much of the southern part of the state. This often rendered dinner conversations filled with in-depth discussions about whose lives are forever changed, who lost their lives, and the traumas left. Complaints from citizens of matters which were not illegal in the first place, such as fireworks going off during Christmas or Fourth of July celebrations.

At first, David had little interest in integrating himself into his family's career choices. The situation was far from a television sitcom of family crime fighters if only that were the case. David's mother, Allison, was a dispatcher for four counties worth of police, fire, and medical agencies. David's father, James, was serving a likely lifetime sentence for sexually abusing one of David's many, many siblings. It was widely speculated that David's father abused more people, David included (of which he had little recollection). It was revealed during the investigation that this was far from his first offense.

This angered David to the point that he swore to quickly end the investigation into his father's crimes. After all, no need to waste prison space on a dead man, right? Because of his parents and the tales of cousins, uncles, and aunts alike, David was well-versed in nearly every aspect of criminal investigation procedure. He was even knowledgeable of court proceedings, often taking full advantage of legal loopholes to advance his interests without bonds. After all, who besides depressed and naive lonely people would take issue with one following their life path? After all, who should care what others do as long as no one is getting hurt? You could say that was precisely the problem.

In a parking lot of a major retail chain store, we find David leaving with a few bags of groceries. Just a typical day, few clouds in the air, a giant of a man paying no mind to those going about their errands. David was the type to park towards the back of the parking lot, furthest away from the store's entrance. He felt it was easier to get in and get out with out the hassle of negligent drivers almost running into him. There was the odd occasion when a teenager would come close to knocking him aside while doing doughnuts in the lot or playing on their phone while driving. This particular day seemed no different. David would occasionally scan the parking lot, usually from him forgetting exactly where he parked or giving a gentle wave to passing children.

On this day, he noticed a young woman on the verge of tears as she tried starting her car, parked five spots from his own. The dim glow of rear lights told David that the woman was likely experiencing some electrical problem, hopefully something simple as a dead battery. As he started to pass the troubled vehicle, another young man, perhaps a couple years older than David, approached the woman and rested his arm against the hood. David could swear he noticed a malicious smirk on the man's face, warranting careful surveillance in the guise of wasting time. It was easy to make oneself seem mindless in public. Stopping to connect a phone to a radio via Bluetooth and check emails would buy enough precious minutes to find the precise moment the use of force was justified.

The woman's car shook as the man was no longer visible from above. David had his moment. Casually he exits his vehicle, tucks his phone inside his pants pocket, and approaches the buoyant Buick. The woman's muffled screaming and the man's loose pants dangling by his knees infuriated David much more. His large hands reached into the car, gripping the man's neck with a paralyzing strength, yanking him from the vehicle.

"What the fuck, you faggot?!" the man cried, "You trying to knock me out so you can fuck me?"

"Alan, I told you that we're done!" the woman cried out, "Why can't you leave me alone!"

"We're done when one of us is de..."

For those paying attention, it is pretty obvious that David was no stranger to these matters. Even more understandable as to why he may possess some "sensitivities" around sexual assault. There are those who try to advocate forgiveness of rapists, sodomizers, and pedophiles; perhaps in some hope of finding them help. Those sorts of "urges" often stem from some trauma. David, though understanding the logic, was not one of these people.

Maybe if one sought help before committing such life-altering atrocities, then he wouldn't be as headstrong in his stance. For this, Alan tried mustering an ounce of strength to cover his bare bottom and barely visible micropenis; the nerves throughout his body began to vibrate. His skin crawled as if a large nest of rather angry hornets tickled his flesh in what would become an agonizing swarm. This sensation urged him to try negotiating his freedom, but David's fingers continued to dig into his throat.

Not only was David particularly sensitive about the subjects of domestic violence and sexual assault, but he was a giant of a man with a short fuse and mystical abilities. By every measure, he was dangerous. By every measure, he was still young, angry, had minimal experience in restraint, and a deserving target in his grip.

His anger seemed to burn into his mind, and the rage fired in his heart. Alan may have been close to death. That is, had David's attention not been deterred by the sudden burst of flames. David seamlessly launched Alan to an empty section of the parking lot to keep the f lames somewhat contained. Now nude and torn with scrapes close to his crotch, Alan paused in an unfamiliar sensation of awe and fright. He was too dumbstruck to begin processing the close brush with death, let alone register the blood seeping from his legs.

David centered his sights on the pant less Alan, his focus drawing so much energy it seemed the wind encouraged a final blow, like an excited stadium audience cheering a gladiator to finish a glorious battle and kill his defeated foe. Static rode the winds, setting off car alarms and flickering lights. David stood between Alan's exposed legs in a blink of an eye. His Sasquatch-like heel hovered over Alan's scrotum, slowly pressing downward. For those who looked on, they might've sworn David took joy in the butchered pig squeals that rang from Alan's lips. The smile that grew with every stomp, each more powerful and swift than the one before, was the earliest indication that David was morphing into some ferocious animal.

Some might've even sworn that they could hear bone being ground into dust, intestines rip ping, and asphalt cracking. As David finally felt he had dealt enough punishment, the adrenaline started to fade just enough for him to realize the screams surrounding him. This was far from the first time he lost control.

For David, however, this was the first time he had felt remorse for doing so. Perhaps, one may argue, it was because David had a previous commitment he was eager to attend to. Having to take time to explain to excited police officers, ready to gun him down, worried David about the impression it may leave on someone he loved. That same someone, and the story which led her to meet David, might've been the same reason David took it upon himself to correct his mistake.

He looked upon Alan, who was mere minutes from a shock-induced coma and bent his body forward. Their faces lingered inches from one another, their breaths intertwining in silence.

"I'm going to do you a favor," David whispered, "Listen close. In moments, it will seem that our encounter never happened. Every injury I inflicted upon you will be healed. You will return to where you stood moments before I set my gaze upon you. You and I will go about our business as if we never met, and it will stay that way so long as you do not give me a reason to find you again. Blink if you understand..."

Alan moaned. His eyelids dragged them selves across the surface.

"Good boy," David added, "Know that while it might seem time has reset, you and I will be the only ones who hold any memory. If you try something like this again, you will have flashes of this. If you ever see my face, even if you catch me in the best of moods, you will shudder at the thoughts that occupy you. And, if I ever find out you have done this again, I will skin you alive and leave your severed head with your eyes in your mouth for whoever still cares about a worthless pile of shit like you. Blink if you understand."

Again, Alan complied with the addition of tears to coat his eyes.

"Good," David sighed.

David moved back just three paces as the colors of his eyes faded to nothing but glowing balls of white light. Space seemed to bend and bubble around him, blurring any and all senses. Slowly, as David said, time seemed to reset itself. David was walking to wards his car with a handful of groceries. The woman, frustrated with her car troubles, is finally able to get it started. Alan, frozen in shock, stands in the parking lot as he processes what he has just witnessed. Someone honked their car horn and waved toward him as if a passing friend was greeting him. It was David, inducing the promised shudder to Alan to wake up from his trance.

"Was that necessary?" a voice crept to David's ear, "You're abusing your abilities."

Alan watched as a faint humanoid white light manifested in the passenger seat of the passing car but scurried off without a word. He had enough excitement in one day. "I know, " David muttered, "But he had it coming."

The white light morphed into an image that could be described only as if David was more androgynous in physical appearance.

"I would be tempted to do the same if in your shoes, but make no mistake, it was wrong to harm him," the Being bellowed.

"Don't take that tone with me!" David roared, "I fixed him!"

"Do you seriously think that is what you did?" the Being asked hastefully, "You merely jumped backward in time. The time line still exists where he dies from the blows you gave him. Do you think that..."

David's eyes flared. "Don't you dare bring her into this!" he screamed.

The being raised his hands in a gesture of surrender, knowing intimately well David was the type to be protective of those he cared about.

"Skye is already nervous about seeing you. You know she's afraid that you will be like her ex," The Being reminded him, "That you would hurt the baby."

"You know damn well I would never bring a kid into it..."

"I know that, brother. In all your life times, a child in danger has always been the one thing guaranteed to bring about your wrath," the Being teases, "Skye wants to believe it. Her heart tells her to move forward, but much like you, her mind still tortures her. I'd hate to see you lose yourself again in front of her when your charms just might be able to help her heal."

His emphasis on the word "heal" sprung a realization into David's mind.

"Are you trying to tell me I can actually heal people?" he asked. "When it is in your heart, yes."

The being jerks his head as if he can hear someone shouting for him. The shift in his face rings something of importance. "Remember what I say, and watch for the lights of eyes in Skye..." the Being muttered before disappearing.

Before David could genuinely comprehend the ominous hint of his visitor, a some what generic rock song rang from his cell phone and car speakers. His finger shakes as he reaches for the call button on his radio and rattles further as he takes a moment for the Bluetooth to fully connect. He reads the digital display as it reveals the caller, his eyes widening with excitement.

"Hello? David, can... can you hear me?" sang an almost equally nervous voice.

"I'm here, Skye," David answered, "I'm just picking up a couple last-minute things from the store."

"Oh, okay!" Skye nodded, "Listen, my plane came in early. I don't mean to rush you, but how long will it take you to get to the airport? I really need to see you."

"Hey, no worries. Give me about fifteen or twenty minutes, and I'll be there," David cracked.

"Okay, okay. I'll, uh, be here then!" Skye laughed, "I love you."

A sudden gasp ended the call before David had a chance to reply. The shock from the words he had just heard almost forced his foot to practically embed his cat's brake pedal into the vehicle's frame. He and Skye had never said those three words to one an other before. Truthfully, the shaking couple was about to meet face-to-face for the first time. Despite the surprise, David managed to churn his nerves into excitement and speed towards the airport. The fifteen to twenty minute window he had promised turned into a five-minute race.

Skylar "Skye" Oliwa was just a year older than David, a gorgeous Polish brunette of high intellect. Sky's grandparents came to the United States as a young couple looking to escape the early days of the second world war, settling on the East coast for work, and had three children while in their mid thirties. The children grew inspired by the times of hardship and their father's stories from when he was both a police and military officer during the war, taking on similar roles in their lifetimes. By the time Skylar was born, most of her immediate family had careers in law enforcement, so she knew little else. A search for justice, sometimes overbearing from family pressures, was in her blood, after all. Wanting to explore herself during and after high school, a dangerous rebellious phase was fostered within her.

During this time, she met and loved a man named Isaac Williams. For reasons Skylar still knew little about, Williams grew violent and possessive. Having developed a dependency on alcohol and illegal narcotics, Williams quickly became a shadow of a man Skye thought she knew. She would eventually be forced to choose her future when she learned that her being the brunt of violent sexual attacks had sown a brand new baby girl.

Skylar had met David through an online anonymous support group for complex post traumatic stress disorder survivors. Skylar, the victim-turned-mother, wanted to channel her family legacy and personal experience into a career as a special agent within the FBI. One of her favorite crime-time TV dramas inspired a preference for behavioral analysis, which David thought was funny as Skye was a practical spitting-image. When it came time for the blossoming couple to reveal each other's faces through a video call, David spawned an almost immediate, child-like crush because he quickly caught on to the resemblance.

What drew Skye towards David was the kinship that sparked from having similar backgrounds. David grew up in a law enforcement family and needed to prove that he was not like his father. He felt an almost supernatural need to be a protector, to help people learn to fight back against the darkness in the world. Skylar wanted to protect her baby from her choice to get involved with Isaac. She grew fearful of how easy it was for her to fall from grace, in a manner of speaking, and wanted to give her daughter the option to be better. Both were conditioned to see the darkness in man but learned to appreciate the light. For both, their kinship was seen as a chance to be the light others needed.

But perhaps they were the light meant for one another?

David's pulse was the only thing he could hear as he scanned through the green-tinted glass windows of the small regional airport. The woman he had waited so long for was now closer than ever, slowly realizing that the man she was eager to meet was standing just outside. Her face morphed into child like glee, almost forgetting her bags as she rushed outside. It was a magical moment, seemingly decorated by nature itself, clouds overhead parted just enough to cast a heart of light around them.

During her stay, Skylar and David split the bill at a hotel in town. David's freelancer schedule offered him plenty of time to spoil Skye in every way he thought imaginable, at least in every way he knew would not be too risky to the baby. From catching a film to hiking a few nature trails to mining for gemstones and fossils, even spending a day at the state capital of Boise for even more fun excursions.

Much to Skylar's surprise, David had one trick up his sleeve. Nearly anyone knowing of the circumstance might not agree with such a move, especially with a child soon to be involved, but David did not care. His youthful excitement and devotion to doing right by this woman rendered him headstrong in his choice. For upon a hill next to a sparkling lake filled with geese and duck, basking in awe of romantics out on the town to celebrate Valentine's Day (and frustrations of men being out-done in front of their dates), David slowly propped himself on one knee. Without a ring in hand but a promise of quality the next time they see each other, David managed to stumble through a question meant to set the foundations of a brand new family.

Much to her surprise, and without hesitation, Skylar squealed and blubbered, "Yes."

Such memories would likely fill entire photo albums or decorative scrapbooks to serve as commemorative gifts for anniversaries or weddings, especially for one like David, who enjoyed taking pictures. But no such evidence exists! After Skylar had gone home to make last-minute preparations to leave DC to move to Idaho, communication suddenly stopped. David grew fearful of the worst that he had been the object of some love affair. David worried that Skye's response to his proposal was all a lie. He grew angry at her and himself for falling for such a pathetic and hopeless trap; eventually, he mustered the strength to distract himself with work to get over his lost lover. Until a moment of silence finally fell upon him.

Months had passed, and the fumes from David's perceived betrayal had finally cleared his mind. But his love could not escape his heart. With this lingering love, he took to the internet and began searching for Skylar's full name. The answers to his questioning came without the need to narrow the results. A news article from Washington DC catches his eye with an obituary attached.

"MAN GUNNED DOWN BY PO LICE AFTER SLAYING PREGNANT EX GIRLFRIEND"

As much as he wanted to deny the truth. As much as he wanted to destroy every thing in sight, the skylight was no more for David. To remember his love, David only had a single picture taken by screenshotting a video call. Skylar did not want David to take any photos of her because she believed the father of her child would try hacking his way into David's life, holding him digitally hostage until Skylar came running back. Skylar also believed someone close to her was relaying everything back to Isaac, even suspicions that a new man was in her life. A plot for vengeance was seeded, and David needed some way to learn more. David also recalled a rather unusual name Skylar mentioned, thinking it to be some hitman for the gangs Isaac associated with. This name would not leave his mind, burning itself deeper with every moment it would arise...

Knightmare.

Chapter 8

The Beginning

MAN GUNNED DOWN BY POLICE AFTER SLAYING PREGNANT EX-GIRLFRIEND

Washington D.C. — A young man was fatally shot by police officers after allegedly murdering his pregnant ex-girlfriend in a brutal act of violence yesterday evening. The victim, identified as Skylar "Skye" Oliwa, was found dead at her apartment in Southeast Washington D.C., while her unborn child also tragically perished in the attack.

Skylar Oliwa, 22, was seven months pregnant when she was reportedly attacked by her former boyfriend, Isaac Williams, 24, during what authorities believe was a confrontation at her apartment complex. Neighbors reported hearing loud arguing and frantic shouting before shots rang out. According to police, after the shooting, Williams fled the scene in a stolen vehicle.

Witnesses who were nearby called 911, prompting a rapid police response. Officers tracked Williams' vehicle to a nearby area, and after a brief pursuit, they cornered him. Authorities say Williams attempted to flee on foot, and when officers ordered him to stop, he reportedly pointed a firearm at them. Fearing for their safety, police opened fire, striking Williams. He was pronounced dead at the scene.

"It is with great sorrow that we report the loss of a young woman and her unborn child," said Police Chief David Jenkins in a statement. "We are continuing to investigate this case, and our thoughts are with the family and friends of Skylar Oliwa during this unimaginable time."

Oliwa, who was known to friends and family as "Skye," had been planning to raise her child on her own after recently ending her relationship with Williams, who had reportedly struggled with violent tendencies in the past. Friends described her as vibrant, full of life, and excited about becoming a mother.

"I just can't believe it," said Rachel, a close friend of Oliwa. "Skye was so excited about the baby. She deserved so much more than this."

Isaac Williams had a history of alleged violent behavior, including prior arrests for domestic disputes. Despite this, he had reportedly been trying to reconcile with Oliwa in the weeks leading up to the tragic event. Authorities are still working to piece together the moments leading up to the fatal shooting.

The case has drawn attention to the ongoing issue of domestic violence and its deadly consequences. Advocates are calling for more attention to be given to warning signs of abusive relationships and the importance of providing support to those at risk.

Williams' family declined to comment, while Oliwa's relatives are left to mourn the loss of both Skylar and her unborn child.

Police continue to investigate the circumstances surrounding the incident.

Chapter 9

A Stage for Aspiring Stars

Big-Time Nightclub Owner Surtar Olsen Brings Opportunity to Boise with Open Auditions

Boise, Idaho — Surtar Olsen, the renowned owner of the multifaceted entertainment hub *Kivuli cha Edeni* (Eden's Shadow) in Los Angeles, has set his sights on Boise for a groundbreaking talent search. In a rare appearance, Olsen will sponsor an open audition event at a local university, offering aspiring performers a once-in-a-lifetime opportunity to impress five major talent agencies. The auditions, scheduled for this weekend, have already generated a buzz in the community and beyond.

A Stage for Aspiring Stars The auditions, which will be held in the university's state-of-the-art performing arts center, are open to singers, dancers, actors, comedians, and other performers looking to break into the entertainment industry. The five talent agencies participating in the event represent some of the biggest names in Hollywood, Broadway, and beyond, making this an unprecedented opportunity for local talent to step into the spotlight.

"This isn't just about finding stars—it's about giving people a chance to shine," Olsen said during a press briefing. "Talent can come from anywhere, and I'm here to make sure Boise has its moment."

Jobs and Lodging for the Chosen Few Adding to the allure of the event, Olsen has announced that anyone accepted by one of the talent agencies will be offered a job and lodging at *Kivuli cha Edeni*. The sprawling Los Angeles venue, known for its luxurious amenities and high-profile performances, will serve as both a training ground and a launching pad for the new recruits.

"Our business is built on fostering creativity and supporting people on their journeys," Olsen explained. "For those who take this leap and succeed, I want to make sure they have a safe and stable foundation as they navigate their careers."

The offer of employment and accommodations eliminates a significant barrier for many emerging artists who might otherwise struggle to relocate and support themselves while pursuing their dreams. Olsen's generosity underscores his reputation as not just a successful entrepreneur but also a champion of new talent.

A Community Uplift The upcoming auditions are more than just a talent search; they're a community event that has already sparked excitement throughout Boise. Local businesses are gearing up for the influx of hopefuls and spectators, and the university is proud to host what could be a transformative occasion for many.

"This event showcases the power of community and opportunity," said Dr. Clara Mendoza, the university's head of performing arts. "It's an incredible chance for our students and local artists to be seen by industry professionals."

How to Participate Performers interested in auditioning are encouraged to register in advance through the university's website, though walk-ins will be accommodated as time permits. Participants should prepare a two-minute performance showcasing their talent and bring any necessary equipment or props. The event is free to attend, and spectators are welcome to cheer on the performers.

An Icon with a Vision Olsen's visit to Boise is part of his broader mission to expand the reach of his talent pipeline and discover untapped potential across the country. His venue, *Kivuli cha Edeni*, has earned a reputation not only for its luxurious offerings but also for its commitment to inclusivity, safety, and community-building.

"I've always believed that great talent deserves a great stage," Olsen said. "This event is about creating those stages and proving that dreams can start anywhere—even here in Boise."

As the weekend approaches, anticipation is building for what promises to be a memorable event. For many aspiring performers, this could be the moment that changes everything. With Surtar Olsen at the helm, the odds of discovering the next big star seem brighter than ever.

Chapter 10

Dream a Dream in Trees

April, 2015.
Boise, Idaho.
A small group of young ladies are nervously walking up the street, through a lo cal university campus. Though still slightly chilly, the weather was nice and people scurried about the city going about their days. This day in particular was special for many young movie star hopefuls, as a producer from a major Hollywood studio was in town, scouting for new talent. A nightclub owner was accompanying him, sponsoring the search and offering both lodging and part-time work at his facilities to help the hopefuls get settled in the Hollywood life style. For the average collage student, looking for a break into super stardom, this was a one-in-a-million shot for dreams.

Among the crowd was 21-year-old Scarlett Argyris, nervously awaiting her turn to audition. The lines were accommodated with interns from the major studio handing out bottles of water and bits of various fruits for snack. As she creeps through the line, watching those leaving the scene in tears, her nerves begin to rattle. In her pocket a playful song started on its own, a ringtone set just for the purpose of identifying Scarlett's older sister, Violet.

Scarlett quickly pulls out her phone to answer, hopeful that her sister would offer words of encouragement in spite of an argument that transpired mere hours before.

'Hey!' Violet squeals over the phone speaker, 'Did you manage to audition yet?'

"No, not yet. They started handing out some snack for those of us still waiting."

'Still waiting? How many people actually showed up?'

"A couple hundred from the looks of it," Scarlett sighed, "Not everyone is a cynic about opportunities like this."

'Hey, I'm sorry about this morning, Scar. It's just- well- the thing just sounds too good to be true! And this nightclub guy, some thing doesn't sit right with him! How many businesses he owns, every single one has had somebody go missing from them! And you've heard the stories about Hollywood guys being fucking creeps.'

"Yeah, I know, but there's also a lot of really amazing people out there too! Don't try to ruin this for me!"

'Scar, Scar...'

"Don't 'Scar, Scar' me! You've always done this! I am done! Don't ever call me again!" Not wanting her feelings towards an unsupportive sister to ruin her shot at stardom, hardly having listened in the first place, Scarlett immediately hung up her phone and set it to Airplane mode to prevent any further calls from coming in. Scarlett and Violet always had a competitive relationship, as most siblings could probably relate.

However to Scarlett, Violet seemed to always overstep her boundaries. Violet seemed to feel as if she was supposed to fill in for their absentee mother, driving Scarlett in sane. Even after moving to the midwest for a new boyfriend, Violet still tried to put her self in that role. Perhaps on a subconscious level Scarlett felt that if she put up with it, maybe something would break through and she could just have a normal sister. But no more. This was her time to break free, to forge her own destiny.

If only she was wise enough to choose a few different final words to her overbearing sister...

Chapter 11

Scarlett's Nightmare

Mystery Surrounds the Death of Violet Argyris in Small Kansas Town

Lawrence, Kansas — Tragedy has struck the small town of Lawrence as Violet Argyris, a 28-year-old woman from Boise, Idaho, was found dead in her home under circumstances authorities are calling "unusual and unexplained." Argyris, who had recently moved to Lawrence to start a new chapter with her fiancé, was discovered unresponsive shortly before a fire engulfed the property late Tuesday night. The cause of her death remains undetermined, with investigators awaiting autopsy results.

The fire, which consumed much of the home, is under investigation by the local fire marshal. "At this time, we cannot confirm if the fire and the victim's death are related," said Lawrence Police Department spokesperson Amanda Kline. "We are pursuing all leads and treating this as a priority investigation."

A Life Full of Promise Violet Argyris was described by friends and family as a vibrant and caring individual with a love for life and an infectious enthusiasm. She had recently announced her engagement and was preparing for her upcoming wedding. Her sudden death has left those closest to her devastated.

"She was everything to me," said Scarlet Argyris, Violet's younger sister, in an emotional interview. "She always pushed me to chase my dreams, no matter how big they seemed. She believed in me when I didn't believe in myself."

Scarlet, 21, is an aspiring actress who has been making strides in Los Angeles after attending an open audition held by major talent agencies earlier this year. Violet had voiced concern about the audition, which was sponsored by a prominent nightclub owner.

"She was so proud of me for going after my dreams," Scarlet said. "But she also warned me to be careful. She said something about it didn't sit right with her, even though I brushed it off at the time."

Scarlet landed the audition and was offered a job and lodging through the agency but ultimately turned it down, choosing instead to carve her own path in Los Angeles. "I wanted to prove to myself and to Violet that I could do it on my own," she said.

Lingering Questions The circumstances surrounding Violet's death have sparked speculation among neighbors and online sleuths, many of whom are pointing to the mysterious fire as a potential clue. Despite the devastation caused by the blaze, investigators believe key evidence may still be recoverable.

"It's too early to draw conclusions," said Detective Ryan Caldwell, who is leading the investigation. "We're conducting a thorough examination and working with forensic experts to determine the sequence of events."

Authorities are urging anyone with information about the incident to come forward as they piece together what happened in the hours leading up to Violet's death.

A Community in Mourning The small town of Lawrence has rallied around Violet's fiancé and family, offering condolences and support. A candlelight vigil is planned for this weekend to honor her memory, with friends and community members expected to attend.

Scarlet, who plans to return to Kansas for the vigil, says she wants to focus on remembering her sister's love and support. "Violet was my rock," she said. "She always told me to dream big, and now I have to do it for both of us."

As the investigation continues, Violet Argyris's loved ones are left searching for answers and holding on to the memories of a woman whose life was cut tragically short.

Chapter 12

The Dragon of Los Angeles

Los Angeles had seen its fair share of chaos—gang wars, political corruption, and unchecked greed. But nothing compared to the night "The Dragon" emerged from the shadows. A figure wrapped in myth and whispers, The Dragon was said to defy logic, wielding powers that bent reality like a sculptor molding clay.

The Sightings Begin

It started small: gang members turning up unconscious in dark alleys, muttering incoherently about walls that moved and shadows that spoke. Security footage from a convenience store showed a fleeting image—a figure cloaked in smoke and fire, moving faster than the eye could follow. The media dismissed it as a hoax, a clever marketing ploy for an upcoming blockbuster. But on the streets, the legend grew.

One witness, a homeless man named Eli, described the encounter to a local podcast:
"I swear on my life, man, I saw it! This guy—or thing—just appeared. The air got heavy, like something was squeezing the whole world. And then... poof! These thugs were gone, just gone. And the walls? They were glowing, like dragon scales."

War on the Underworld

Over the next months, Los Angeles became a battlefield. Drug shipments vanished mid-transit. Arms dealers found their warehouses reduced to smoldering craters, yet with no evidence of explosives. The city's most feared crime syndicates were turning themselves in, their faces pale and haunted.

Detective Sofia Moreno of the LAPD was tasked with investigating the phenomenon. Moreno, a pragmatic woman who didn't believe in ghost stories, was baffled by the sheer absurdity of it all. Her reports described scenes that defied reason:

- **A gang hideout where walls had melted into glass, reflecting infinite copies of terrified men.**
- **A nightclub where time itself seemed frozen, patrons locked in a silent scream as The Dragon moved through them like a phantom.**

- And most chillingly, a series of burnt symbols etched into the ground—ancient sigils no linguist could decipher.

Theories Run Wild

Speculation ran rampant. Some claimed The Dragon was a rogue government experiment, a soldier enhanced with forbidden technology. Others whispered of an ancient protector awakened to cleanse the city of its sins. But conspiracy theorists went deeper.

Online forums buzzed with theories about The Dragon being a byproduct of an interdimensional rift—a rift allegedly opened during a secret military operation in the Mojave Desert. They pointed to leaked satellite imagery showing unusual energy readings near Los Angeles.

A group of amateur paranormal investigators even claimed to have tracked The Dragon to a forgotten subway tunnel beneath the city. They live-streamed their descent, only for the feed to cut abruptly. Days later, their gear was found at the site, melted and fused into grotesque shapes. Skeptics believe the so-called "paranormal investigators" staged the incident in order to gain internet virality.

The Dragon Speaks?

One night, a hacked broadcast interrupted every television and phone in Los Angeles. The screen displayed a single image: a burning dragon, coiled around the city's skyline. A distorted voice followed:
"You have poisoned this city. I am the antidote. Those who spread corruption will know my wrath. I am the flame that cleanses. I am The Dragon."

The message sent shockwaves through the city. Whether it was truly from "The Dragon," or someone feeding into the legend remains unclear. The Dragon wasn't just a myth; it was real—and it had a purpose.

The Final Showdown

The climax came during a gala hosted by the city's wealthiest elite, many of whom were rumored to be connected to criminal enterprises. As the guests sipped champagne and exchanged secrets, the air shifted. A low rumble echoed through the hall, and the lights dimmed.

The Dragon appeared—a towering figure shrouded in smoke and shimmering heat. Time seemed to distort as guests fled in terror, only to find themselves back where they started, as if reality itself were looping. The Dragon spoke no words but extended a hand, and the room erupted into chaos. Walls twisted into serpentine shapes; chandeliers became glowing orbs of fire.

Detective Moreno, present at the gala undercover, confronted The Dragon. In the ensuing standoff, she managed to fire a single shot. The bullet stopped mid-air, melting into liquid metal before falling to the ground.

"Why?" she demanded, her voice trembling.

The Dragon turned its burning eyes toward her. "Because no one else will."

With a roar that shook the earth, The Dragon vanished, leaving behind only ash and the sound of flames.

The Aftermath

In the days that followed, Los Angeles was eerily quiet. Crime rates plummeted, and many of the city's most powerful figures disappeared, their fates unknown.

Moreno continued her investigation, but every lead dissolved into dead ends. The sigils remained a mystery, and witnesses spoke only in hushed tones. Yet, deep in her heart, she knew The Dragon wasn't gone. It was waiting, watching, ready to strike again when the city's darkness returned.

As the legend of The Dragon grew, so did the fear—and hope—that Los Angeles had found its protector, one who wielded powers beyond human comprehension.

Chapter 13

Alternate Realities

Mysterious Man Claiming to Be from Alternate Universe Disappears in Denver

Denver, Colorado—A bizarre and unsettling mystery is unfolding in Denver after a man claiming to be from an alternate universe suddenly vanished without a trace. The man, who identified himself only as "Dr. Elian," captured the attention of locals and authorities with his extraordinary story of apocalyptic chaos, supernatural battles, and enigmatic beings he called the "Vergobretus."

Elian first appeared in a downtown Denver park two weeks ago, disheveled and agitated, insisting he had been "tricked" into leaving his world by the Vergobretus and "Division Theta", whom he described as powerful and deceptive entities. Witnesses said he spoke with an urgency that was hard to ignore, detailing an alternate reality on the brink of destruction.

A World Torn Asunder

According to Elian, his home world was a dystopian nightmare where supernatural forces clashed in catastrophic battles, tearing society apart. "It's not just war," he reportedly told one listener. "It's a total collapse—ghosts, demons, and things you can't even imagine ripping the land and skies apart."

Elian claimed that humanity in his universe had been reduced to fractured pockets of survivors, many of whom turned to desperate measures to endure. Despite the chaos, he spoke of a glimmer of hope in the form of a mysterious figure named Dakota Frandsen.

The Mysterious Dakota Frandsen

In his tale, Dakota Frandsen was a man of legend in Elian's world, leading a resistance against the apocalyptic forces. Frandsen, Elian said, worked alongside extraterrestrial allies, forming an unlikely coalition to save what remained of civilization. "He's not just a man," Elian had told a group of onlookers. "He's a symbol of hope, and he's fought battles no one else could survive."

Elian described Frandsen as enigmatic yet unwavering in his commitment to finding solutions, no matter how unconventional. "He's the only reason the end hasn't already come," Elian had stated.

A Sudden Disappearance

Elian's unusual claims quickly drew curiosity—and skepticism—from the public and media. Authorities attempted to interview him, but he refused to provide identification or other details, maintaining his story of being from another reality. Onlookers reported that he appeared to be in distress but otherwise coherent.

However, just as suddenly as he had appeared, Elian vanished. Witnesses at the homeless shelter where he had been staying said he walked outside late one evening, muttering about being "summoned back." He was never seen again.

Surveillance footage from nearby cameras showed nothing out of the ordinary, fueling speculation about whether Elian's disappearance was voluntary, coerced, or something more mysterious.

Unanswered Questions

While Elian's claims have sparked debate among conspiracy theorists and paranormal enthusiasts, law enforcement remains cautious. "At this point, we have no evidence to support his story, but his disappearance is unusual," said Denver Police spokesperson Clara Reyes. "We are continuing to investigate."

Some have drawn parallels between Elian's story and local folklore about interdimensional beings, while others dismiss it as an elaborate hoax. Still, those who met him are left with lingering questions.

"He seemed terrified, but not crazy," said Martin Hayes, a Denver resident who spoke with Elian. "It was like he knew things he couldn't possibly know. Maybe he was telling the truth."

A Tale for the Ages

Whether a modern myth or a glimpse into a hidden reality, Elian's story has left Denver abuzz with speculation. Was he truly from an alternate universe, or was he a troubled man seeking attention? And what, if anything, can be made of his warnings about the Vergobretus and the mysterious Dakota Frandsen?

As the search for answers continues, one thing is certain: Elian's brief time in Denver has left an indelible mark, sparking conversations about the unknown—and reminding us that sometimes, the strangest mysteries are the ones that walk among us.

Chapter 14

StarCulling

It all started with the dreams—haunting, vivid visions that felt like they belonged to someone else, yet I knew, deep down, they were mine. In these dreams, I glimpsed a world far beyond anything I could imagine. Across an endless expanse of stars, through the folds of time itself, there was another version of me. She lived among beings that defied explanation—creatures whose existence seemed impossible within the confines of our reality. Some were almost human, their unearthly beauty both captivating and unsettling. Others had faces like horses or lizards, with wings so vast they cast shadows that seemed to writhe with life. And then there were those I couldn't even begin to describe—forms that bent logic and words to their breaking point. Surely, they couldn't be real... could they?

The dreams refused to be ignored. Night after night, they returned, more vivid and relentless, leaving me shaken and questioning everything I thought I knew about the world. I tried to share them with my family, desperate for understanding, but how could they possibly grasp it? These weren't childhood fantasies or fleeting curiosities. They were something deeper. Dreams didn't leave you breathless, drenched in sweat, after sprinting through alien landscapes. And they certainly didn't leave you waking up with scratches on your arms after fighting what could only be described as a mutant dinosaur in your sleep.

Now, at 27, life is its own chaotic whirlwind. I'm married to Jacob, my high school sweetheart, and we're raising three beautiful daughters. Our oldest, Mariah, just turned four, and between moving into a new house and planning her birthday party, my days are packed. There's barely room to think about those dreams anymore. But they linger, hiding in the quiet moments, waiting to remind me they're not truly gone.

One night, that fragile normalcy shattered. A piercing scream tore through the stillness of the house. Jacob was away at a conference, and I was home alone with the girls. My heart raced as I ran upstairs, dread gripping me tighter with every step. I found Mariah trembling under her blankets, her little face streaked with tears. "Mommy! The dragons want me!" she sobbed, her voice trembling with fear.

Dragons? For a moment, I wanted to dismiss it as a child's nightmare, but something about her words struck me cold. I held her close, whispering comfort as I stroked her hair. Her small body quaked in my arms, and it took what felt like forever to calm her. Then, in a whisper that froze me to my core, she said, "The monsters want you too, Mommy."

Later, she brought me her notebook—a tattered spiral-bound pad she carried everywhere. Page after page was filled with drawings of creatures that mirrored the ones from my childhood dreams: dragons, strange humanoid figures, and beings that defied explanation. How long had these nightmares haunted her? And how had I missed the signs?

Panic settled deep in my chest as questions flooded my mind. Was this just coincidence? Some shared, strange quirk of our genetics? Or was it something darker—something I couldn't begin to understand? I wanted so desperately to protect her, even though I had no idea how.

In desperation, I called my mom, hoping for guidance or at least some reassurance. Instead, she brushed it all aside with a dismissive laugh. "She's probably just got an active imagination. You did too, remember? Maybe you should consider medication, just in case."

Her words infuriated me. Medication? For my little girl? How could she reduce this to something so trivial when I knew there was more to it?

As I hung up, the phone buzzed with an incoming call. Jacob. Relief washed over me as I answered, his voice instantly grounding me.

"Deme, is everything okay? I saw Mariah screaming about dragons on the baby monitor."

"Jake..." I trailed off, glancing at Mariah, now curled up on the couch with her notebook.

"This isn't new," he said gently. "You've been having nightmares again too. I think we need help."

"I'm not medicating her," I said firmly. "There's something real happening here."

"I know," he replied, his steady tone giving me pause. "But there's more. Deme, my dad... he appeared in my hotel room. He told me you and Mariah might be in danger."

"What?" The words barely made it past my lips. "Jake, your dad's been gone for two years."

"I know," he said, his voice cracking. "But he was here, Deme. And he warned me."

My thoughts spun in a whirlwind of disbelief and fear. A warning from his dead father? What could this mean?

Jacob's voice broke through my spiral. "Do you remember Will from school?"

"Will? There were a lot of Wills."

"You know which one," he insisted.

Big Will. Of course. The boy everyone teased relentlessly for his height, but who never let it crush his kind, quirky spirit. Over the years, his fascination with the supernatural had grown into something more—ghost hunts, TV appearances. Rumor had it, he'd made a career out of it.

"If anyone can help, it's him," Jacob said. "We need to reach out."

He was right. If anyone could make sense of this madness, it was Will. After tucking Mariah back into bed, I opened my laptop and started searching. Was he still in town? Still chasing the paranormal? Would he even remember me?

Before I could get far, a sharp knock at the door startled me. Through the window, I saw a black SUV idling outside. Unease crept through me. Before I could react, a sharp sting in my neck sent the world spiraling into darkness.

When I woke, I was in a room that looked like a luxury hotel suite—plush furniture, a flat-screen TV, even a mini-fridge. But the deafening silence whispered the truth: my children weren't here.

Panic clawed at my chest, and just as I was about to scream, a woman's voice came through the TV. "Mrs. Mindiler, please remain calm. Your children are safe. Mariah and June are in our Pre-K play area, making friends as we speak."

The screen flickered to show a children's playroom, where Mariah and June laughed and played. But as my vision adjusted, I saw the toys... moving, as though guided by their thoughts. My stomach twisted. How was that possible?

"And Jeanne," the woman continued, "is in our nursery. We detected early signs of pneumonia and have taken steps to ensure her comfort."

The image shifted to my youngest, peacefully resting in a state-of-the-art crib, surrounded by monitors tracking her health. My fear deepened, and my resolve hardened. Whatever was happening, I had to get my children back.

"Is... is she okay?" My voice trembled as I spoke, my eyes catching on a camera perched just below the television screen. It looked out of place, like an unwanted guest, a reminder I wasn't entirely free in this moment.

"She's doing well," the woman replied, her face now fully visible. She had the kind of look you'd expect from someone in charge—poised, calm, but with a hint of weariness in her eyes. "How are you feeling, Mrs. Mindiler?"

"Where am I?" I panted, the fear clawing at my throat and making it hard to breathe. "Can we answer that first, please?"

She tilted her head slightly, her expression softening in what I could only hope was sympathy. "I understand your confusion, and for what it's worth, I sincerely apologize for how you were brought here. It was not our intention for you to be taken in such a manner. You were supposed to come willingly. When we discovered that our operative acted... prematurely, we had to move quickly to ensure your safety and that of your family. We've done our best to create a safe, comfortable environment for you to recover. This facility offers top-notch childcare, education, job training, and medical care—courtesy of some very generous benefactors. Your room is equipped with state-of-the-art entertainment, gaming consoles, and complimentary room service. Everything you might need."

"That's great and all," I snapped, unable to keep the edge out of my voice, "but seriously—where am I, and why is my family here?"

"Please, Mrs. Mindiler, try to remain calm," she said, her voice steady yet insistent. "I'm getting to that." She took a small step closer, her hands folded neatly in front of her. "You and your family are here because this facility specializes in monitoring and supporting unique individuals such as yourselves. Think of it as a top-secret program—not the kind you see in spy films with harsh interrogations and experiments, but one that prioritizes health, development, and well-being."

Her careful words didn't ease my anxiety. If anything, they only made it worse. I leaned forward, my fists clenching the blanket beneath me. "You're dancing around my question, and it's not helping my fears!"

She sighed, her expression tightening for just a moment. "The dragons you dreamt about as a little girl—the ones Mariah dreams of too—they aren't just figments of your imagination. But I think you already suspected that, didn't you?"

Her words hit me like a bolt of lightning. My breath caught, and my eyes widened. My reaction betrayed the truth I hadn't even admitted to myself.

"Before you were brought here," she continued, her tone unwavering, "you were searching for an old classmate—William Goldblum. Correct?"

I swallowed hard, my voice barely above a whisper. "Yes..."

"He was one of our most skilled students. Many like him are brought to facilities like this one across the globe to receive advanced training in their unique abilities."

"Training for what?" I demanded. "War?"

The woman paused, her gaze never leaving mine. "If you choose to stay, you'll learn more about what's truly happening in the world. You'll discover that you are far from alone in this. But know this—our world is on the brink of a crisis. The best among us are working tirelessly to make sense of it, but time is running out. Training individuals like you to unlock the abilities buried deep within you may be our last hope to prevent further tragedies like the one that brought you here."

The television flickered suddenly, drawing my attention as it cut to a series of news reports. The screen showed chaos in Los Angeles. Headlines described a vigilante terrorizing the city, whispers of police corruption, and even rumors of superheroes. At first, I thought it was some sort of prank—the footage looked like it belonged in a blockbuster movie. But then, a headline caught my eye: *"Dragon Strikes LA Penthouse, Police Uncover Prostitution Ring."*

I leaned forward, my stomach knotting. "Wait... you're telling me the Dragon in Los Angeles is real?"

"Your husband's fascination with the subject wasn't misplaced," she said carefully. "The Dragon is an anomaly—a being with abilities unlike anything we've ever encountered. It's a person, a man who's troubled past and subsequent rage manifested almost god-like potential. That's why finding people like you is critical. The Dragon represents everything we're trying to avoid: chaos, desperation, rage. We believe celestial souls like yours and Mariah's are part of a larger evolution. With time and training, you could help create a new future—one that avoids the pitfalls that gave rise to the Dragon."

"Celestial souls?" I repeated, my voice shaking. "What are those?"

"Deme," a familiar voice cut in, making me spin around. Standing in the doorway to the bathroom was Jacob, his shoulders slouched and his eyes darting nervously. He looked like a child bracing for punishment. "They're starseeds," he said quietly. His tone was filled with a mix of guilt and uncertainty. "And I... I'm the one who contacted them about you and Mariah."

My jaw dropped. "Why would you do that, Jacob?"

"Please, hear me out," he pleaded, tugging at the collar of his shirt like it was choking him. "It seemed like the only way to get you real help. Plus... I thought it'd be like a fancy family getaway."

My eyes narrowed as I spotted something on his neck—a faint needle mark. Some patches of his skin even looked scaly and red, as if he had an allergic reaction to whatever was in the injection. My stomach turned. "They drugged you too?" I asked, my voice breaking, "It looks like you are having a reaction, baby."

The woman—Margaret, as I would later learn—stepped forward again. "Once more, I deeply apologize for the methods used to bring you here. Your husband has been check out and the irritation you see should subside soon," she said. "I'll understand if you choose to leave. But before you make that decision, there are a few final details I'd like to go over, if that's all right."

Jacob moved to my side, guiding me back toward the bed. His touch was steady, but I could feel the tension in his fingers. "Go ahead, Margaret," he said, his voice low and resigned.

Margaret straightened, her tone becoming more formal. "We know you'll have questions—many of them. Myself or one of my colleagues will always be available to assist you. Additionally, your room's video library contains comprehensive guides to every aspect of the facility." The television screen shifted again, now displaying an index of instructional videos. "The sections highlighted in green cover emergency protocols—fire, extreme weather, active shooter scenarios, and so on. While this facility is highly secure, we believe it's always better to be prepared."

My eyes scanned the titles: *In the Event of Fire. In the Event of Extreme Weather. Active Shooter Protocols. Terrorist Threats. Cyber Intrusion.* Each one felt like a chilling reminder that no place, no matter how advanced, was ever truly safe.

And here I was, standing on the precipice of a truth I wasn't sure I wanted to understand.

"If you'd like, you're welcome to spend a week exploring the facility at your leisure," Margaret began, her voice calm and inviting. "During that time, you can observe everything we have to offer. Take a look at the childcare centers where the little ones thrive, sit in on the classes designed for our teenage and adult members, and enjoy the amenities available to all residents. Personally, the pool and garden are my favorite spots. They're perfect for relaxing and reconnecting with yourself."

She paused, letting her words settle before continuing. "If, after your observation period, you decide to stay, you and your family will be fully enrolled in our programs. Thanks to the generosity of our benefactors, your home will be cared for during your absence. The utilities and upkeep will be maintained, and compensation for your time here will be deposited directly into your bank accounts. We want to ensure that you can focus on yourselves without external stressors."

Margaret's smile grew softer, a small touch of understanding in her expression. "If, however, you decide this isn't the right fit for you, a private escort will ensure you and your family are safely transported home. No pressure. No needles. I promise."

I turned to Jacob, my husband and rock, searching his face for any sign of doubt or reassurance. "What do you think, Jake? This feels... I don't know. Too good to be true."

He met my gaze with a steady expression, his voice low but firm. "Deme, I've done a lot of research about this place and other little conferences. Read testimonials, watched interviews, and even walked through parts of what I could easily get to myself. I wouldn't have brought us here if I didn't think this was the best option worth considering," He exhaled and placed his hand over mine. "Maybe we should give it a chance."

Margaret nodded approvingly, taking a small step forward to bridge the space between us. "It's entirely up to you. The facility is designed to be fully accessible to our guests, with the exception of certain employee-only areas for safety and operational reasons. The only time access would be restricted to you would be during an emergency, and even then, our instructional videos will explain everything you need to know."

She gestured toward the sleek television unit mounted on the wall, her tone becoming more matter-of-fact. "As for security, your rooms are equipped with electronic locks programmed specifically for you and your family. Maintenance and security teams do have override access, but only when absolutely necessary, such as in the case of a medical emergency or technical issue."

Margaret's gaze softened as she addressed a concern I hadn't even voiced. "And about the camera you noticed below the television—it's part of the gaming console setup, not a surveillance device. I understand how it might look, but our privacy policy is incredibly strict. The instructional videos available to you will also guide you through ways to ensure that your boundaries are respected during your stay here."

She stood back slightly, clasping her hands together in a poised but approachable manner. "Now, before I leave you to discuss things, do you have any questions for me?"

I crossed my arms, narrowing my eyes. I'd heard all the reassurances, but the skeptic in me wasn't ready to let go just yet. "Why should we trust you? Or this place? For all we know, this could be some elaborate scheme."

"Deme!" Jacob nearly jumped from his chair, his voice quick and pleading. "Please, not now."

Margaret raised a hand to calm him, her composure unshaken. "It's okay, Mr. Mindiler. I understand where your wife is coming from," she said, her voice warm and empathetic. She turned her attention back to me, her eyes meeting mine with quiet strength. "Let me explain. From one mother to another."

The screen flickered to life, displaying an image of Margaret sitting beside a hospital bed. In the bed lay a young boy, his face pale and gaunt, hooked up to a myriad of machines. Margaret's voice softened, and for the first time, I detected a slight tremor in her words.

"This is my son, Darik. A few years ago, I was in a desperate place. He was suffering from a rare autoimmune disease that caused multiple organ failure, and I couldn't find anyone who could help us. We tried everything, but every option seemed to hit a dead end." She paused, her hand briefly brushing the edge of the photo frame in her lap.

"Then, I heard about this facility. They were conducting experimental treatments with promising results. I had nothing left to lose, so I brought him here. It wasn't an easy decision. It wasn't an easy process. But now..." Her voice broke, and she took a moment to collect herself.

Margaret's lips quirked into a faint, bittersweet smile. "Now, he's thriving. In fact, he just started teasing me just a couple hours ago about having a girlfriend."

The screen shifted again, this time displaying a live feed of the children's play area. A much healthier Darik was standing in the center of the room, a radiant smile on his face as he hugged a small girl—Mariah. The sight of my daughter laughing and playing so naturally was enough to make my chest tighten with emotion.

"She's too young to have a boyfriend!" David suddenly exclaimed, his protective instincts kicking in as he leaned toward the screen, his expression a mix of humor and exasperation.

The room filled with quiet laughter, the tension lifting slightly. Even I found myself smiling despite the whirlwind of thoughts in my mind. This moment of innocence, of normalcy, felt like a lifeline.

Maybe this place wasn't so bad after all. Maybe it was a chance for us—a chance for something better.

"I think... we'll take the week," I said softly, still unsure but willing to take a leap. "We're here anyway, and Mariah seems to be doing so well. It'd feel wrong to take that away from her."

Jacob's face lit up, his smile wide and genuine. "I'm glad you said that," he replied, excitement threading through his voice. "We've got a few hours before picking up the girls. Why don't we take a tour and see what this place really has to offer?"

I nodded, my anxiety slowly unraveling with each passing moment. Together, we explored the facility. The classrooms for adults were fascinating, ranging from lessons on psychic abilities to courses on more practical skills like budgeting and communication. The childcare facilities were bright, colorful, and filled with laughter.

But it was the garden that stole my breath. It was lush, vibrant, and impossibly serene—a mix of tropical plants and fragrant flowers that seemed to come straight out of a dream. The air felt clean and warm, like stepping into a slice of Eden. Margaret later explained the presence of snakes, carefully introduced as part of the ecosystem's natural pest control.

Throughout our tour, we met other families who had chosen to stay. Each one shared stories of hope, healing, and personal growth. Their enthusiasm was infectious, and I found myself slowly, tentatively, beginning to believe that maybe this place could offer us something extraordinary.

Later that evening, an announcement over the overhead speakers informed us that the afternoon Pre-K class had ended and it was time to pick up the children. Jake and I made our way to the childcare section of the facility, and along the way, we crossed paths with Margaret, who was heading to pick up Darik. She struck up a conversation about the programs and how the children seemed to flourish, developing into prodigies with remarkable ease.

Seizing the moment, I asked about the extensive safety protocols and why they were deemed necessary. Margaret admitted she had wondered the same thing when she first started working there. She explained that the most significant incident during her tenure had been a small fire caused by a faulty microwave, which was quickly contained. No one had been hurt, though she chuckled about the understandable spike in everyone's blood pressure. Her superiors, however, believed it was better to be overly cautious, citing the network of these facilities that had existed as far back as the 1940s.

The mention of that era sparked fleeting thoughts of conspiracy theories about Nazis and UFOs—something Will would undoubtedly have a field day dissecting. But those musings quickly faded as Mariah and June barreled toward Jake and me, their laughter bubbling over as they wrapped us in excited hugs. Their energy was infectious, their faces glowing with joy from the day's activities. Baby Jeanne was brought out shortly after by a nurse, looking healthier and happier than ever. The nurse reassured us that Jeanne was fully recovered but advised us to keep a watchful eye on her for a little while, just to be safe.

Margaret's reunion was equally heartwarming as Darik ran up to her, his little arms wrapping tightly around her legs. With a goofy grin and puppy-dog eyes, he asked if he could have a playdate with Mariah later. Jake, ever the protective father of three young girls, hesitated before sighing deeply and giving a reluctant nod.

By nightfall, under the clearest, most breathtaking sky I'd ever seen, I found myself wondering if this place could truly be our new home. Mariah and Darik had their playdate which further blossomed an obvious puppy love relationship between the two. Baby Jeanne's stimulation proved effective enough she started to surpass the first two years of a child's developmental milestones overnight. As the days passed and my family grew more comfortable—more at ease—among the other residents, I realized I didn't even want to go back. This wasn't just a facility; it was a sanctuary. It was luxurious. It was paradise.

It felt like where we truly belonged.

On the final day of our trial week; Jake and I sat with our three girls on the master bed in our living space, awaiting for Margaret to come on the television screen to ask the fateful question. Will we be staying, or will we return to our normal lives? Anticipation grew. The dawn of a new age for our family was entering into our hearts and hopes; only to be stripped away by a painful, repetitive screech, alarms, and spinning red lights. Large metal slabs covered the main door into the living space and windows. Then, the screams filled the outside halls in a Hellish symphony of agony, fear, and gunfire.

"Warning, unauthorized personnel have been detected, active shooter protocols engaged," shouted a mechanical voice over, *"Guests, please make your way to the nearest escape elevator. This is not a drill."*

In the center of the room, a trap door opened to reveal a solid metal container as it rose to the ceiling. A split down the middle opened, revealing the same futuristic elevator shafts I saw in the safety videos. Instead of an empty shaft, large enough to fit a group of ten, inside stood one man dressed in all black armor. He was large, muscular, rugged in what little of his flesh we could see; even without the weapons he carried he was intimidating. I gripped baby Jeanne tight, as Jake held Mariah and June close. The man stepped out of the elevator, silent as approaching Death, stalking his next kill.

I took a look into the glimmers of blue in the man's eyes, the rage subsiding into sadness the moment the realization came over us both.

"Dammit, Deme," he whispered, "I hoped it wasn't true."

"Will?!" I gasped, "What the hell are you doing?!"

"Jake's dead, Deme. So are your daughters."

My heart raced as I watched will take his hand from the grip of his gun and place a finger over a speaker near his left shoulder. I could feel my family panic, wondering if we were about to die at the hands of someone we thought we knew.

"Believe me, I prayed that you wouldn't be in this shithole. I prayed you somehow escaped. Even if you don't believe me now, answer me this," Will stated as his stance shifted into aggression, "When did they have shark teeth?"

Jake, Mariah, June, and even Jeanne uttered this reptilian hiss in unison. Their faces contorting, twisting, skulls becoming more pronounced; they were the dragons from my dreams! Will shoved his finger into the speaker on his shoulder, triggering a high pitched tone sequence. My family, whatever they were, all leaped into a feral rage; Jeanne biting and ripping skin from my should as I threw her across the room.

"Get in the elevator and run!" Will screamed as he opened fire.

Adrenaline taking over, blood running down my arm, I listened to the only source of familiarity in the fogs that surrounded me. I ran inside the elevator, slamming my hand into the emergency override switch meant to help shut the elevator doors faster in the event a threat was moving in too quickly. Will fought hard against the monsters, killing the things that pretended to be my daughters by completely decapitating them. With mere inches left for the door to close, the thing pretending to be my husband lunged forward and got his head stuck. He teeth looked more human, his eyes pleading for help as the metal tightened, the bones in his crumbling under his skin as Will's brute strength rips the rest of his body back into the room. I was left with the creature's severed head, its skin turned into scales and its eyes a faded yellow with slits for pupils.

This was Hell. How could I believe this was paradise? How could I have been so stupid! Why did I get trapped in this mess?! Why me?! Was this all a facade?!

The elevator stopped into an underground bunker, others who managed to escape trying to gather together and process the horrors unfolding above us. Margaret spots me through the crowd, rushing to my side as I collapsed to the ground. Everything I knew was gone, the only thing keeping my heart beating is the sting remaining from the animal wound I thought was my daughter.

"Mrs. Mindiler! Mrs. Mindiler!" Margaret screamed as she shook me, "Demetria, where is your family?"

"Monsters," I choked, "They became monsters!"

I felt all the eyes in the bunker look to me, every pulse stopping at the realization of what I said. Soon, they all begin to scream themselves, drowning the final warning playing over hidden intercoms in the bunker.

"Cleansing protocol initiated."

The smell of chemicals and gasoline filled the bunker just moments before the fire torn and burned the flesh of the remaining survivors. The smell of vomit temporarily dousing flames for mere moments before the flames entered our airways and burned us all from within.

"These were the memories I could scalp from just one of the victims of the genocide at the Celestial Soul facility outside Los Alamos, New Mexico; at least from her spirit. By all accounts, it seems someone has tried their best to cover up the events at these facilities ever since the invaders tried to liberate the unsuspecting victims. Many who joined in the assaults, like the William Goldblum from Demetria's account, also perished in the battle. I have done my best to chronicle their struggles, reaching out to what families were left behind. But, much like the story of the Mindiler family, they are left to records of mysterious disappearances. This 'Margaret' that spoke on behalf of the facility seems to even lost her son in the conflict. I've tried my best to warn others in New Age of UFO groups but the masses blindly silenced them because they were deemed "not high vibration." I swear these zealots only are into the escapism behind the alleged disclosure movement. They do not care about the innocents dying. They do not care, or

even acknowledge these people. Greedy pigs. My search will not end. I need to head to Los Angeles to find this 'Dragon" figure. I don't think he is some monster, but a man out for vengeance. He'll be the key to making Knightmare pay for his crimes."

-The Red Widow

Chapter 15

Truth and Reconciliation

My heart sank the moment I got the phone call about the latest kills. Each loss cut deeper than the last, a grim reminder of how many innocent lives were being destroyed in this fight. It felt like the weight of the world rested on my shoulders—a world I'd vowed to protect, yet one that seemed to slip further into chaos every day. When I came to Los Angeles, I was a man consumed by vengeance, driven by a singular purpose: to make those who thrived in darkness pay for their sins.

"One fight. One enemy. One war."

That mantra burned in my mind like a brand. It began the moment I lost Skye. Her death became the defining moment that clarified everything. My mission was no longer just about survival or justice—it was personal. Kill Knightmare. That was the goal. Nothing else mattered.

At first, my actions were precise, methodical. Guided by intel and the vivid, haunting visions that plagued me, I tore through the streets like a storm, uprooting criminals and exposing corruption. But as time went on, I began to see how deep the rot went in this city—how far it extended across the globe. It wasn't just about one villain or one syndicate. This was a machine, a vast network of power, money, and lies that reached into every corner of society.

I didn't hide who I was or what I had become. I kept my circle small, ensuring that only a few knew my identity. The whispers and rumors about a mysterious figure in the shadows were deliberate. I wanted fear to work for me, turning my presence into a myth, an urban legend whispered on darkened streets.

By day, I could pass for just another man. A tall, imposing figure, sure—enough to make some people nervous—but nothing extraordinary. I moved through crowds like a ghost, unnoticed and unremarkable. But at night, I became something else entirely. Fear was my cloak, my armor, and my weapon. Those who lived in darkness knew to fear the figure that moved among the shadows, silent but relentless.

Of course, there were those who saw through the mask. Detective Angelo Masuka was one of them. He called me about the dead girls, dragging me into the case. Angelo and his partner, Debra Carpenter, had discovered my presence in Los Angeles months earlier after I intervened in a horrific domestic incident. A man, high on meth, had tried to kill his teenage daughter after she flushed his stash. I didn't kill him, but I made sure he wouldn't hurt anyone again. Now permanently paralyzed, his scars were now breathing warnings of the demons which would feast upon him given the opportunity.

No one in the apartment building admitted I was involved. Fear kept them silent, and my unique abilities ensured that no cameras captured my face. Surveillance footage glitched, recordings disappeared—it was as if I had never been there. Angelo and Debra, however, weren't fooled. In time they broke protocol to provide me with information on suspects they couldn't touch regarding other cases, driven by the same frustration that fueled my crusade.

Their frustration was justified. In Los Angeles, justice was often bought and paid for. Prosecutors ignored mountains of evidence, knowing that pursuing cases would overwhelm the already overcrowded prison system. Especially when it came to pedophiles. Those with money and influence could make their problems disappear with a simple bribe. The system was broken, and everyone knew it.

Then there were the disappearances—major traffickers and drug lords vanishing without a trace. Some were my doing, but not all. It seemed others had joined the fight, though their motives were far from clear.

Copycats emerged, twisting my actions into something almost religious. To them, I was a vengeful Messiah, a savior cleansing the city of corruption. Others were darker, more methodical. Their actions bordered on the ritualistic, as if they were devils mocking my efforts. It was unnerving, knowing that my war had inspired both saints and monsters.

Rumors began to swirl that I wasn't alone—that others like me had risen from the shadows. One name kept appearing in the whispers: the Red Widow. She had been sending me intel for weeks, exposing secret facilities tied to disappearances inf UFO disclosure movements and New Age cults and horrifying experiments. According to her messages, these facilities were responsible for feeding the missing into a vast, genocidal machine. Her last message claimed she was coming to Los Angeles to meet me. If anyone could convince me they were truly "like me," it would be her. But I needed to see her up close to be sure.

Amid the chaos, Gregory Mills became an unexpected ally. We'd crossed paths during a rescue mission, and somehow, he managed to break through my walls. I don't know how he did it, but his presence became a lifeline. He was a mentor, a confidant, someone who helped me hold onto the fragile threads of my humanity.

I wasn't blind to how the world saw me. To many, I was nothing more than a brutal vigilante, a ghost who haunted the city's underworld. Gregory's support groups, filled with survivors and witnesses, only confirmed that image. 1 person can confirm an angelic figure—someone who looked like me—has tried to warn me against the dangers of my path and the repercussions of my tactics. I hadn't seen this figure since arriving in Los Angeles, but the thought lingered in my mind.

Gregory, however, was different. He wasn't just a voice of reason; he was my anchor. He reminded me of what truly mattered: humanity. It wasn't about vengeance or power. It was about protecting those who couldn't protect themselves, about fighting for a world worth saving. Perhaps I should attend one of the support groups he hosts, I'm apparently a highly demanded guest. Scarlett would probably be there after the mess at the diner—a spitting image of the woman I lost, setting me on my warpath.

What's her part in this? Why can't I shake her?

As I scoped the perimeter of the crime scene, waiting for Masuka or Carpenter to spot me, these questions and more filled my mind as I tried to understand the next move. What was it about? Why was this place, these victims, targeted? As I was lost in thought Carpenter managed to sneak up next to me, giving me a proper fright her playful smirk pierced the fogs of my mind.

"Some superhero you are," she joked, "You're lucky I know you're one of the good guys."

"Safe to say I'm not sure what that even means anymore," I admitted, "What's the situation?"

"Straight to fucking business as usual... that's not healthy man. Especially with walking shit buckets doing fucked up shit like this," Simmons ranted, "Seven dead. Three males, four females, one of which was likely transgender from the look of things. Records show one additional female, a Jacquelin Pantazis, lives at this residence but no one can seem to locate her. Neighbors were the ones who found the bodies, they were an elderly couple who had to be taken in for heart attacks and likely a few broken bones. A secondary neighbor saw the old couple go down, came to rush to their aid, then nearly had a coronary while on the phone with dispatch trying to describe everything."

It was hard for me to maintain a pokerface at the description of the crimescene. The crowds of concerned neighbors, paramedics, police, and forensics investigators made it impossible to sneak by and without a clear picture of the brutality waiting inside I couldn't just teleport in without risking potential contamination. I wanted in there, especially knowing there was a message left. Knightmare had to know who I was, know that I would come looking.

"So, does the mighty Dragon want a look inside?" Carpenter probed, "We've got maybe five minutes before the press swarm the place."

I nodded, "Let's go. I'll exit out of the back if things get too dicey."

"Betcha say that to all the girls!" she smirked.

I had hardly known Carpenter to make it through a singular sentence without some sort of expletive or innuendo. Whether these were byproducts of her career choices, or just her personality, I hadn't had the pleasure of knowing her long enough to know for sure. Most cops I knew took on a darker sense of humor to cope with the stressors of the job, probably the only line of defense they had against a plunge into alcoholism. But still, Debra had a certain charm about her which rendered her colorful tones into a fun personality quirk rather than a walking HR violation.

No, I did not sleep with her. Though, truth be told, I probably would not be against the idea.

The building we approached seemed to have a dark haze about it, a figment of the horrors inflicted upon the innocent lives lost. Call it the psychic equivalent of clawing one's final words into any nearby surface, when you know opportunity of salvation has turned away. These mists, the smells of spoiled pork, the canvas of oxidized blood, and the severed heads neatly arranged side-by-side with their eyes gouged out and resting upon their tongues. The remains all situated to permanently face the message written in victims' blood.

Drip. Drip. Come and Play.

"Pretty fucked up, ain't it?" stated Masuka, "Any idea what this sick bastard is trying to say?"

The sinking feeling in my chest had just one idea. Torture.

"I think it's a booty call," Carpenter chimed, "Someone clearly wants to fuck and fuck hard."

"You're not totally wrong," I muttered, rolling my eyes, "The person who did this sees this as nothing more than playing a game."

"Who the fuck would think this is a game?" Masuka asked.

I glared towards him, answering his remark,

"Oh," he retracted, "So, what else can you tell?"

"Depends on where the bodies are," I muttered, "And where the final victim is..."

From the corner of my eye, I noticed the hazed image of a young woman standing in a doorway leading towards a hallway. The look in her eyes was of horror, disgust, and looming rage.

Masuka, recognizing the look, waved his hand in front of my face to pull me from the trance and asked, "Any chance you're seeing a 5'3" goth girl?"

"Yep," I answered, "And she's acting a bit weird... like I had something to do with her death."

A brightly painted van sat parked outside the apartment building, its gaudy design clashing with the gritty, urban setting. The camera crew spilled out, already zeroing in on my location like vultures circling a carcass. I took a deliberate step back, every muscle tense as I imagined my body splitting into atoms and blasting through the nearest wall, leaving nothing but empty air behind. My instincts screamed to leave, but curiosity rooted me just long enough to overhear Carpenter's voice cutting through the chaos.

"They haven't told anyone yet," he muttered, his tone grim. "The bodies tied to the skulls—still missing."

Missing. Of course they were. They weren't going to turn up. Not intact, anyway. Those bodies weren't casualties; they were pawns in some sick game. A game I wasn't sure I understood yet, but one I couldn't ignore. Each piece seemed to add another layer of questions with no clear answers.

When I finally pulled myself out of the moment, I let the tension fall away and allowed my form to shift, phasing out of the scene. By the time I rematerialized in a safer space, the facade I'd been holding together—the one the public saw, the one that played the part of a grounded, rational man—was already crumbling.

I'd spent too much time running blind, chasing scraps of information on the streets, hoping for a lead. It was pointless. The answers I needed weren't out there; they were buried in the details of those people's lives. Why were they chosen? What lured them into that trap?

I made the call to stay in for the rest of the day. My 15th floor apartment, while far from a sanctuary, offered enough security to let me breathe and regroup. The building was nestled in a quieter part of Los Angeles—quiet for L.A., anyway. It wasn't luxurious, but it was well-equipped: security cameras, electronic entry codes, even a roving guard on some nights. For the price, it was a steal, especially considering it came with neighbors who minded their own business.

The real selling point, though, was the studio space. A previous tenant had turned one of the larger rooms into a recording studio, complete with soundproofing and high-end wiring. I'd repurposed it into my own personal war room. A ten-gallon fish tank in the corner provided a rare moment of calm when I needed it, though I rarely had the luxury of downtime. Most days, the room was cluttered with maps, notes, and screens displaying data I didn't dare trust to the cloud. This was where I charted courses, predicted movements, and planned every move like a chess game with my life on the line.

Someday, I told myself, this space could be something else. Something creative. Something meaningful. Skylar and I had talked about that—building a studio for music, or maybe art. But dreams like that felt distant, almost alien, these days. With each passing battle, I couldn't shake the nagging doubt that the man I'd been for her might just be a mirage, a version of myself I was losing to the war.

The hum of my devices pulled me out of my thoughts. A quick glance at the clocks told me it had been just over twenty-four hours since the shootout at Carrie's Diner. In that time, eight socialites who'd only been looking for a night of fun were now dead. That fact sat heavy on my shoulders.

Why them? What made them the targets? And why did Jacquie seem to blame me for her death—if she was even dead? The eyes, too—they kept flashing in my mind, an unanswered question I couldn't push aside.

I turned to my laptop, hammering away at the keys. Jacquelin Pantazis had to be the key. I pulled up everything I could find on her—her background, her family, her friends, her relationships. Her digital footprint was small, but what I uncovered told a bleak story. She wasn't a social butterfly. In fact, she kept to herself, avoided large crowds, and from what little I could glean, struggled with self-harm. She had all the markers of someone vulnerable, the kind of person predators zero in on. But something about this didn't fit the usual patterns. This wasn't just some scumbag taking advantage of a broken girl. It was bigger than that.

I'd been at it for nearly an hour when a new email lit up my screen. The sender? Red Widow. They had been writing me for a couple weeks now, with no indication that they were to be interpreted as an enemy. I also wasn't sure enough to label them an ally, either. It was through this "Red Widow" I learned that the disappearances of New Age followers and ritualistic murders of major drug lords were connected to hunt for Knightmare. Exactly how, it was unclear, but the threads remained. As I was tearing into the criminal underground of Los Angeles, someone or something was stepping up their influence.

I sighed. The last thing I needed was another distraction. But the subject line caught my eye, telling me this was another clue my mysterious companion generously was gifting me: *"What fuels the fires in Eden's Shadow?"*

Curiosity won out, and I opened it. What I found sent a chill down my spine. The email was packed with intel: notes on a rumored genocide at a classified Los Alamos facility, reports of hybridization experiments involving Non-Human Intelligence, and details of supposed reptilian shapeshifter feeding grounds. But the real gem was the surveillance footage.

The video showed Jacquelin Pantazis at a nightclub, approached by a sharply dressed man as one of the victims scurried away. His frame was large, broad-shouldered, much like mine. But his face was blurred, frustratingly out of focus. The timestamp on the video placed Jacquie and her friends at the club around 10 p.m., two nights ago.

My mind raced. The state of the bodies suggested they'd been killed in the early morning hours—around 3 a.m. That gave me a timeline, but it also raised more questions. Who was the man in the video? Why had he singled out Jacquie? Was she just easy prey, or is there something else?

I had to make a call. There was a lingering anxiety filling my chest, my pulse ringing in my ears, knowing the tides of Knightmare's Game were shifting beneath my feet. Such open displays of brutality, there was no more hiding. All the major players were about to come into the open and it was going to be bloody. With the various clues provided by Red Widow, I had to contemplate the possibility this fight was not going to be central to just one world—one plane of existence—but many.

I reached for my cell and dialed Masuka's direct line, my foot pummeling the floor beneath me in anticipation.

"This is Masuka," he prattled.

"It's Dragan," I shook, "Are you still at the scene?"

"Affirmative, I need to make this quick," Masuka responded, "What did you find?"

"Jacquie is most definitely deceased. Where her body may be, I honestly have no idea, but I have video confirmation she was at Eden's Shadow before her disappearance."

"Woah, woah, woah, seriously?" Carpenter interrupted, "How did you get that?"

"Apparently, I have a groupie, no fucking clue who the hell it is, that just sent me surveillance footage from inside the club that shows Pantazis being approached by a larger male subject who seems to really mind his appearance. The angle of the footage blurs his face but the timestamps out this literally hours potential time of death."

In the silence, the seductiveness of the tension, I took the video file from Red Widow's message and forwarded it to Masuka's and Carpenter's department emails. I knew it was going to be their request, it was part of our arrangement into combating the criminal underground; total information exchange. The matters involving the secret facilities and extraterrestrial connections were all mine, for now. Los Angeles already had enough on its plate with Hollywood's perverted grips.

"David, I just saw you sent an e-mail, this the video?" Masuka asked.

"I figured you'll need to get back to work," I joked, "I'll give you guys a call first thing if I find anything else."

"Copy that, good job," Carpenter remarked, her professional tone stepping in.

Once the line disconnected, I set my phone on my desk and laid back in my office chair, just wanting a moment to process everything. The darkness that seemed to creep around the corner felt like mere precursors to an inevitable escalation. The haze of a young woman, an early causality of this war, lingered before me with tears staining her eyes. I had to address her, she wasn't just some figment of my imagination.

"Jacquie, I presume?" I asked her.

The ghostly woman nodded her head, fear still plaguing her heart.

"Is there a reason you're unable to talk?"

Whether it was through my mind's eye, or Jacquelin's efforts, her image became clearer; and so did the horrific truth behind her demise. The haze around her spectral form was likely a manifestation of her final thoughts in life to hide the wounds who naked body endured. Jagged cuts all over, bruises, even teeth marks of someone much larger than her branded an animalistic brutality upon her very soul. They were likely why she couldn't talk.

"I see. Can you show me what happened?" I asked her, "I want to help you."

I could see Jacquelin's throat quiver, her lips shake, and her body tremble as she reached for the hand I extended out to her. She still had such hesitation. I tried to keep calm, telling myself I had nothing to do with it and this endeavor was just complicated by the lingering trauma of what happened. Having actually heard my voice, seeing me make the active effort to directly address her, it allowed for a proper bridge between us to be built. This was a chance to uncover the truth and set her free.

At least, until there was a buzz at the door, and Jacquelin faded into the night.

"So close," I mumbled under my breath, "But who the hell could that be?"

I hurried to the front door, another buzzer urging me along. It was getting to be too late at night for a social call, I never got any visitors, food deliver and I would always meet with police at a public location. So, who the hell was bothering me now?

I approached the door, my feet silent against the floorboards. Through the wooden door, I could hear a faint breathing stammered by nerves. I could tell it was female, smaller in stature, and she had a sense of doubt about her being in that very spot. I took a peak through the peephole, which was covered by a small metal plate, finding myself unable to steady my pulse when I realized the surprise waiting outside as I slowly opened the door.

"Scarlett?" I asked, "What... how did you find this place?"

Scarlett seemed conflicted, almost fearful of my judgment. Who could really blame her? After all she's seen only a fraction of my abilities, likely heard even more fantastical stories, and against any shred of common sense she still sought me out. That alone spoke volumes about who she was as a person, and that this was far from some social visit.

"Hey, um Pas..." Scarlett swallowed to steady her voice, "Pastor Greg gave me this address. I'm sorry if I'm bothering you. I just... after what happened at the diner... I... just wanted to talk."

The poor girl was shaking, unsure of how I'd respond. In her anxieties I sensed proverbial walls up around her heart, something happened to her to draw her to me. Her pulse beat against the bricks, only becoming strong and steady enough to break through the moment I extended my arms out to Scarlett to embrace her; it seemed like the only meaningful gesture to let her know she was safe here.

"Why don't you come in and take a seat," I whispered to her, "It's getting late."

"Are you sure?" she asked, "I don't want to be a bother."

"No, no, you're not a bother," I assured her, "I figured after we met at the church this was going to happen at some point."

She nodded, wiping the tears from her eyes with the sleeves of her hoodie as she took a seat on my couch. From the corner of my eye, I watched as she detailed my apartment, trying to get a better understanding of who she was dealing with. Her focus seemed drawn to one particular photo I had sitting on a side table by the couch; a moment of happiness and love captured from an eternal life ago. I could tell right away she noticed the similarities, twisting strands of her own hair between her fingers as a nervous tick.

From the kitchen, I made my way to the refrigerator and shouted, "Would you like anything to drink? Sweet tea, soda, juice?"

"Some tea, with ice, if that's okay?" Scarlett yelled back.

"You got it."

From the sight of Scarlett at my door, I knew the conversation to come would not be easy to handle. Providing something to drink was a way to allow both of us to relax, the simple act providing the same relief as if the glasses were filled with alcohol. While the allure might've be understandable, in order to keep my senses in peak condition and avoid mishaps, I avoided drinking alcohol on a regular basis. Maybe on a special occasion, or whatever amounts may be in cold medicine, I will let some pass my lips. With my life, as it has evolved, it seemed I was deemed unworthy of those joyous moments years ago.

But still, I knew how to be a good host when need be.

As I scooped some ice from my freezer part of my fridge, poured the drinks, I made every effort to keep my composure when I walked into the living room. I handed Scarlett her drink and took a seat a the opposite end of the couch.

"The picture on the table, here..." she stammered, "Is that Skylar?"

I nodded, "So Greg told you about her, did he?"

"Was it supposed to be a secret?" Scarlett started to panic, "I didn't mean to intrude. It's just..."

"He told you that he wouldn't be surprised that, at the diner, the way I acted towards you was because how much you looked like my fiance," I interrupted, "And now that you saw her picture, you see it too?"

Scarlett took a sip of her tea before letting her head sink, gently nodding.

"I'll be honest, seeing how much you looked like Skylar was a pleasant surprise," I chuckled, "Hell, if you had an East Coast accent ... I'd probably think you were her somehow back from the dead! And boy, I would have been in trouble!"

I couldn't help but laugh as memories flooded my mind of Skylar's face whenever she'd seen me pull off one of my "miracles." Whether it was making flowers literally bloom in the palms of my hand, healing cuts or burns she sustained from how accident prone she was, or using my mind to let her fly; her eyes always seemed to grow in amazement. She was the first person to see me for all the good I could do, the one who made it so I felt human and happy. The rains of my longing for her started to be free from my eyes. Soon followed by the showers of hope she still saw the good in me and hopeful showers that she'd find forgiveness in her heart for what I had become.

"She sounds like such a beautiful soul," Scarlett commented, "What happened to her?"

"She was," I sighed, taking a moment to collect myself, "The official story was that her ex raped and killed her. What made that news hard was that she was also about six months pregnant with a baby girl who didn't make it. Police ended up gunning her ex down. The circumstances around the incident were still being investigated, but not much else was ever found."

Scarlett scooted herself closer to me on the couch, trying to offer a bit of comfort when she realized the emotional depth of what she'd asked. "Is that why to came to LA?" she asked.

"In a way, yes. Skylar's ex, her daughter's biological father, was a drug runner. Skylar once told me about a guy that was being talked about quite often by her ex and the lowlifes he ran with. She thought it might've been some hitman, and if something were to happen to her, this man likely had something to do with it," I explained, my teeth gritting as I told the story, "Knightmare."

Scarlett bit her lip as if a thought suddenly occurred to her. She reached into her purse, that resting on my floor, and pulled out what looked like an old diary. Some the edges seemed burned, like it was a priceless heirloom rescued from a burning building.

"When I heard you say that name back at the diner, I knew I had to find you," Scarlett explained as she quickly moved through the pages, "Shortly after I went to an open audition, back home, my sister died in a fire but... something just didn't add up. In her diary, on the day of my audition, she said she had a nightmare the night before and that I was going to be hurt. All she could remember was the word, *Knightmare*."

I looked in the diary as Scarlett held it open, flashes of her sister's fateful day flooding my mind. Scarlett may have had the answer to a question I was looking for. In the excitement I dug through every resource showed her everything I had on Knightmare, the various operations tied to him, the estimated millions he's killed. The realization of the connection we shared, what brought our paths together was filled with tension and excitement; confusion and liberation; love and war. The flames of our excitement getting the better of us, we found ourselves tangled in skin and serenaded by the creeks of my queen-sized bed.

The sex was intense, the passion overwhelming, and the sensation of primal human connection seemed mythological. But, in that moment, Scarlett and I realized we were no longer alone in our nightmares. Falling asleep while our bodies remained interlocked, our skin seemed to glow in the dead of night.

By morning, the night of liberation was taken from us. Scarlett freed herself from my embrace to find the restroom, barely conscious enough to maneuver the strange apartment, only to return to the bedroom screeching unholy terror. Her fear awoke me from a dead sleep, adrenaline coursing through my veins when I saw the source of it all. One woman's severed head, resting on the ledge just outside my bedroom window, eyes scoped out and left on the tongue. I pulled out my phone to call the authorities, moving closer to the head, and realized who the victim was.

Jacquelin Pantazis...

Scarlett ran for the bathroom, her fears forcing her body into pushing her intestinal contents through her lips as if she had been poisoned. The game was now personal, as hinted by the faint message left next in blood on the window.

"Come and play, brother."

www.ingramcontent.com/pod-product-compliance
Ingram Content Group UK Ltd.
Pitfield, Milton Keynes, MK11 3LW, UK
UKHW041316100125
4051UKWH00026B/146